COLLECT THE S

Boffin Boy and the Inva[illegible] from Space
1 84167 613 6

Boffin Boy and the Wizard of Edo
1 84167 614 4

Boffin Boy and the Monsters from the Deep
1 84167 615 2

Boffin Boy and the Red Wolf
1 84167 616 0

Boffin Boy and the Lost City
1 84167 617 9

Boffin Boy and the Time Warriors
1 84167 622 5

Boffin Boy and the Red Wolf
by David Orme

Illustrated by Peter Richardson

Published by Ransom Publishing Ltd.
Rose Cottage, Howe Hill, Watlington, Oxon. OX49 5HB
www.ransom.co.uk

ISBN   184167 616 0
        978 184167 616 6
First published in 2006
Copyright © 2006 Ransom Publishing Ltd.

Illustrations copyright © 2006 Peter Richardson

A CIP catalogue record of this book is available from the British Library.

Design & layout: *www.macwiz.co.uk*

Find out more about Boffin Boy at *www.ransom.co.uk*.

Boffin Boy
AND THE
Red Wolf

By David Orme

Illustrated by Peter Richardson

Ransom

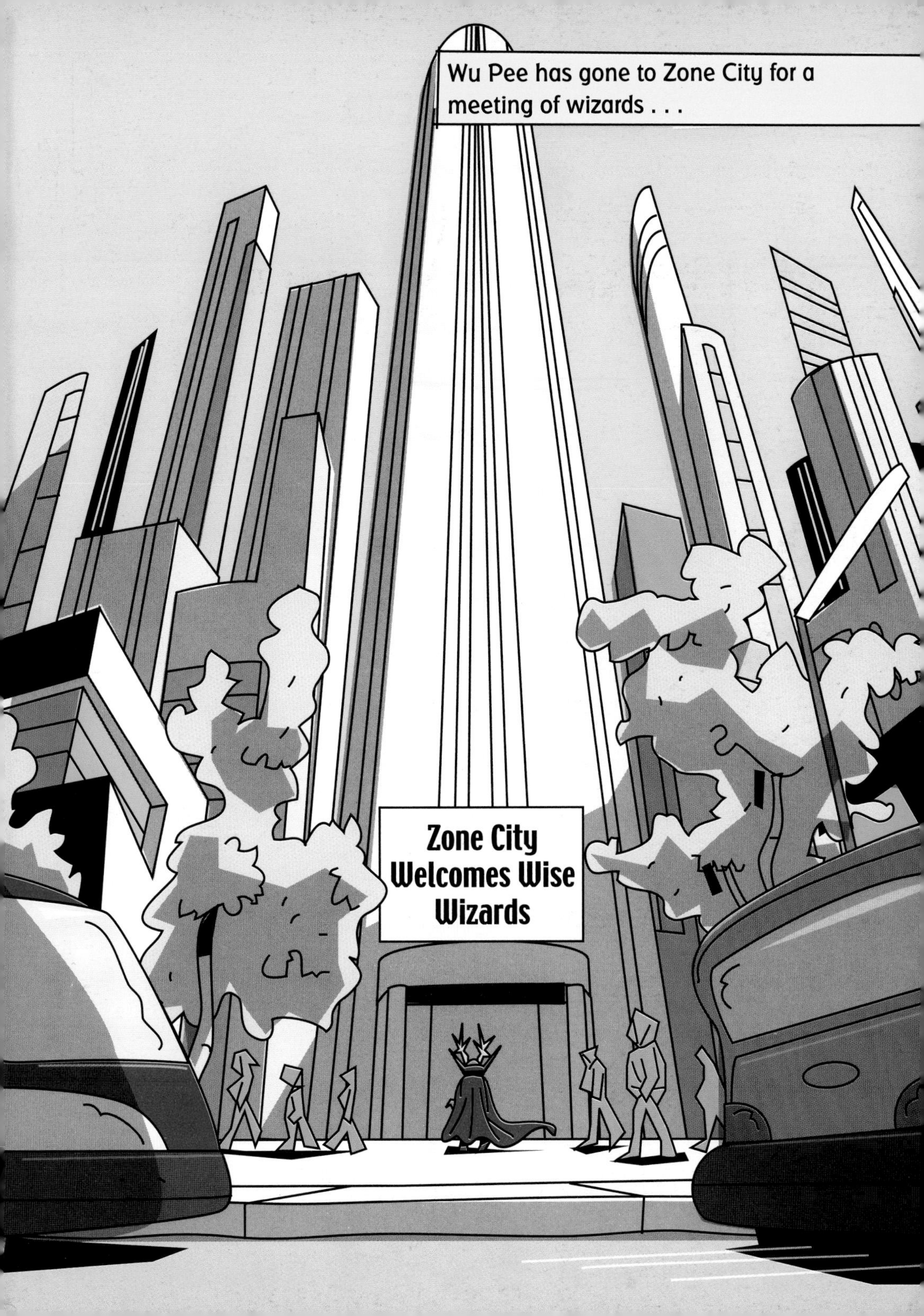
Wu Pee has gone to Zone City for a meeting of wizards . . .
Zone City Welcomes Wise Wizards

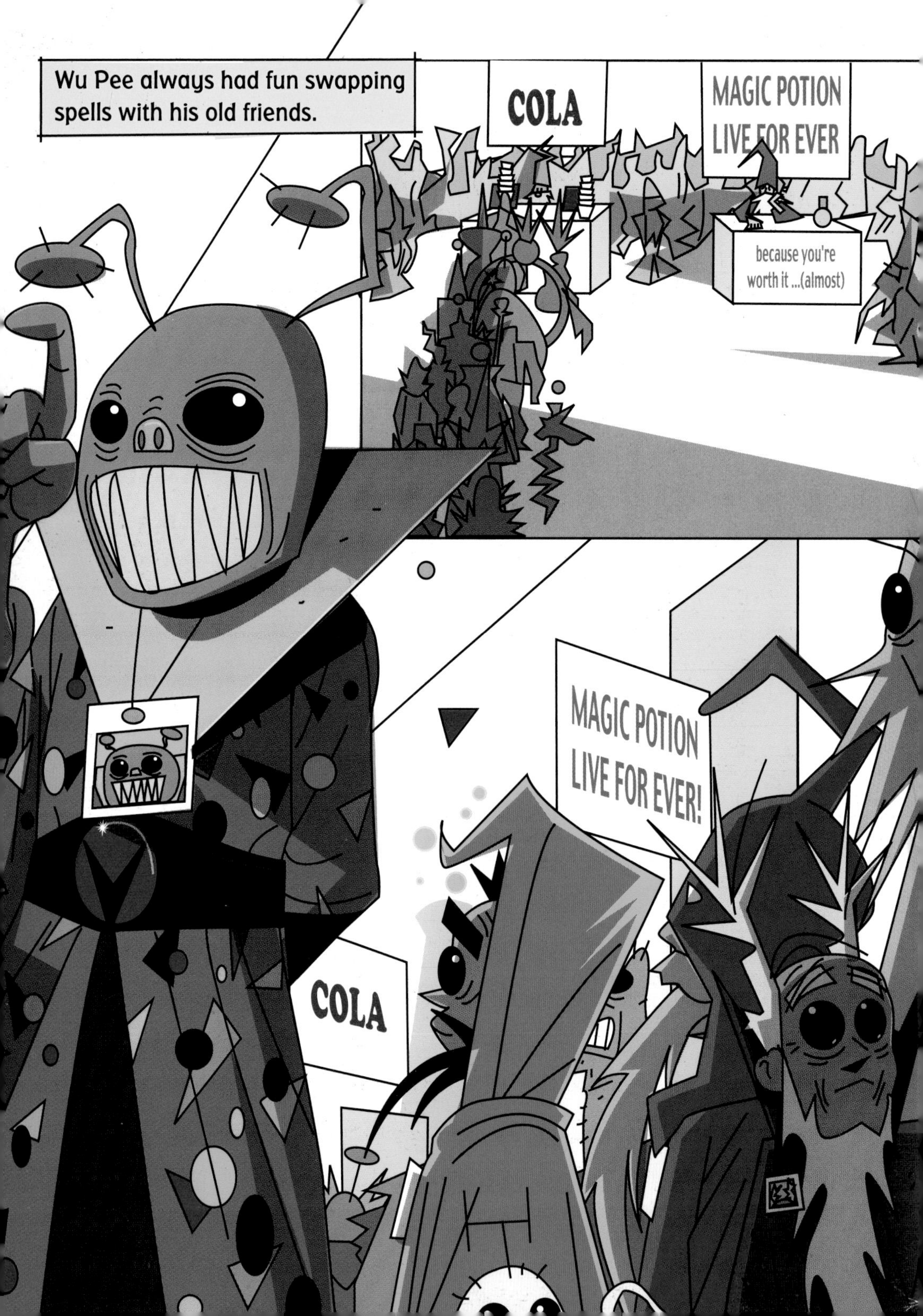
Wu Pee always had fun swapping spells with his old friends.
COLA
MAGIC POTION
LIVE FOR EVER
because you're worth it ...(almost)
MAGIC POTION
LIVE FOR EVER!
COLA

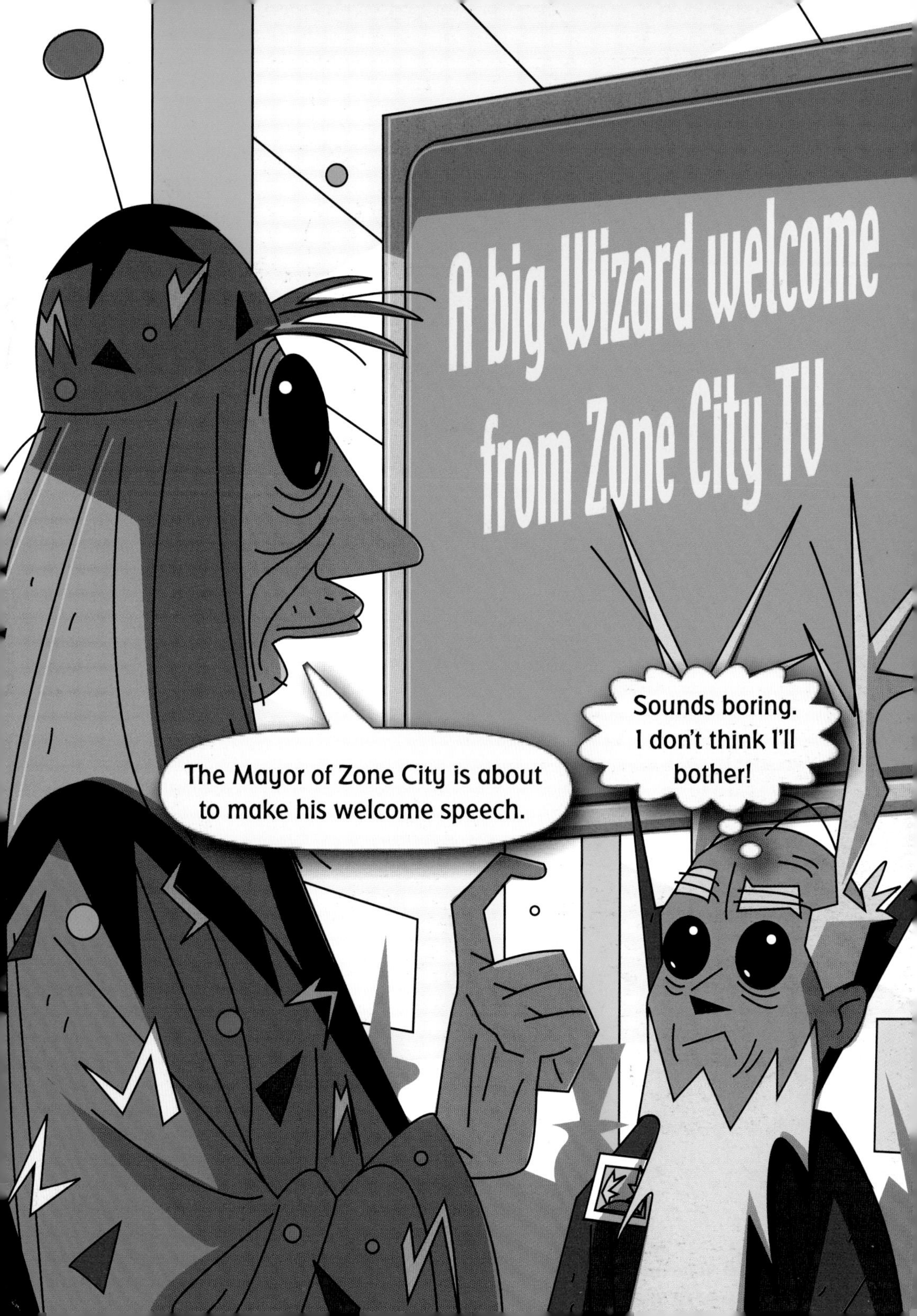
A big Wizard welcome from Zone City TV
The Mayor of Zone City is about to make his welcome speech.
Sounds boring. I don't think I'll bother!

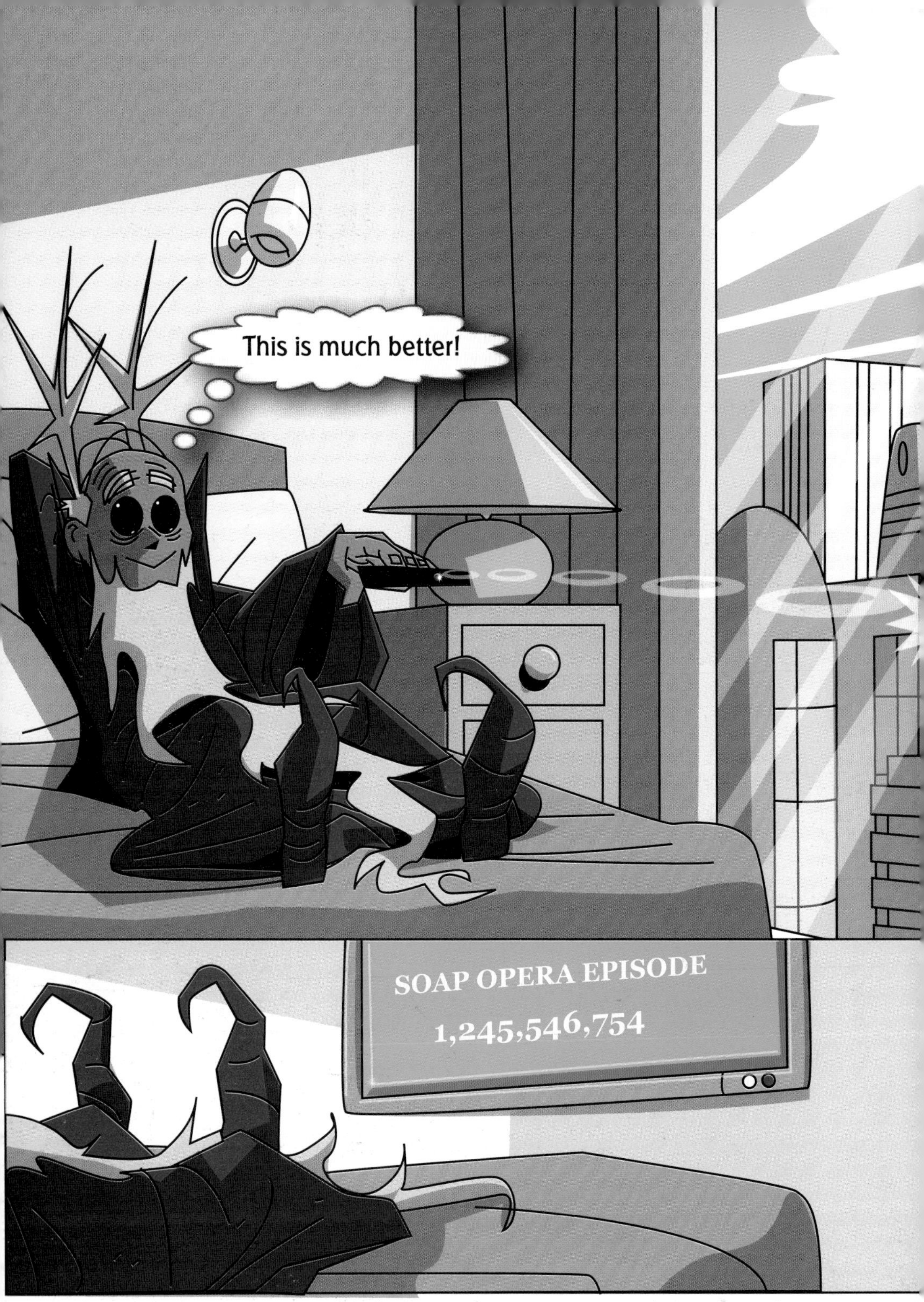
This is much better!
SOAP OPERA EPISODE
1,245,546,754

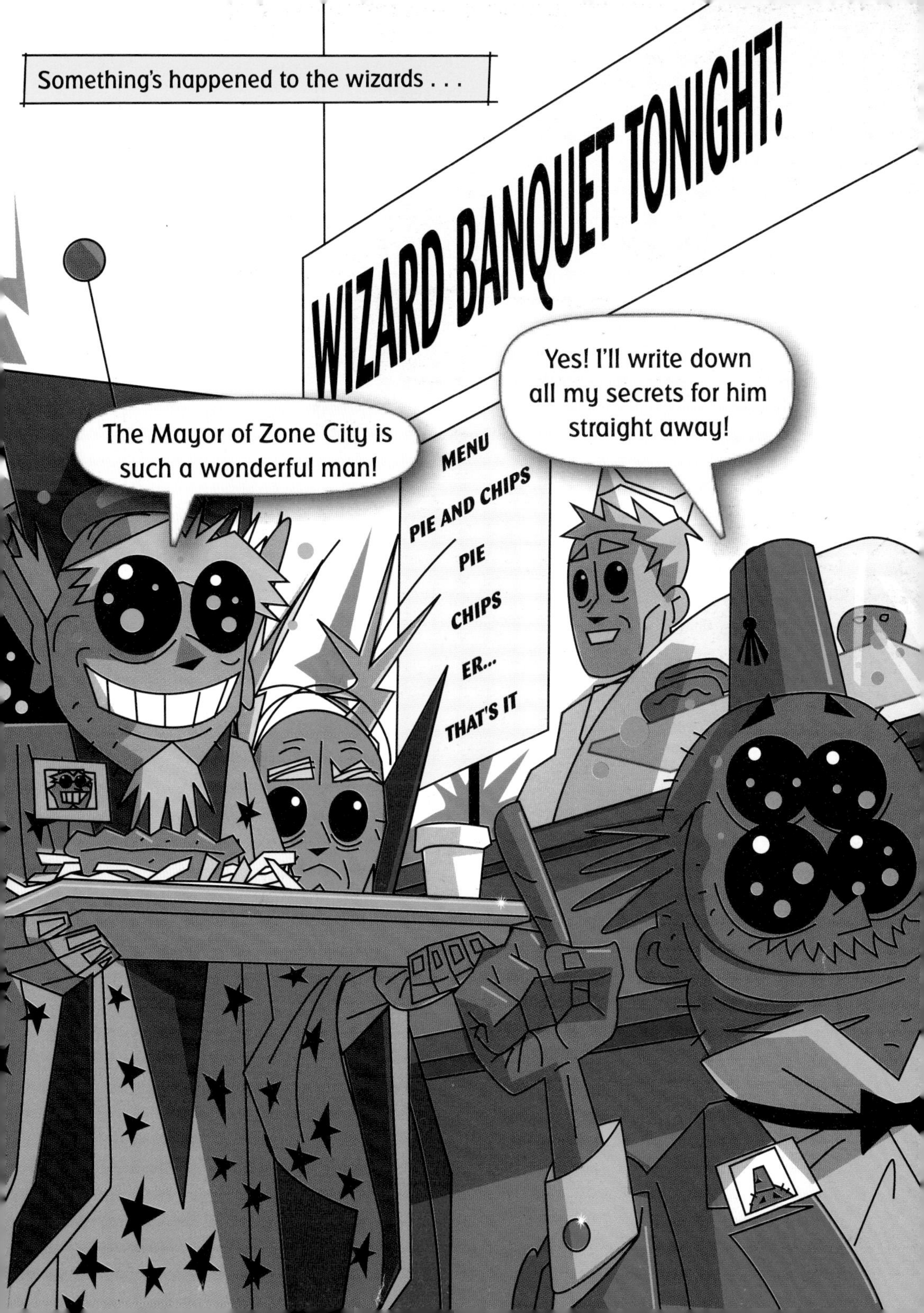

Something's happened to the wizards . . .
WIZARD BANQUET TONIGHT!
The Mayor of Zone City is such a wonderful man!
Yes! I'll write down all my secrets for him straight away!
MENU
PIE AND CHIPS
PIE
CHIPS
ER...
THAT'S IT

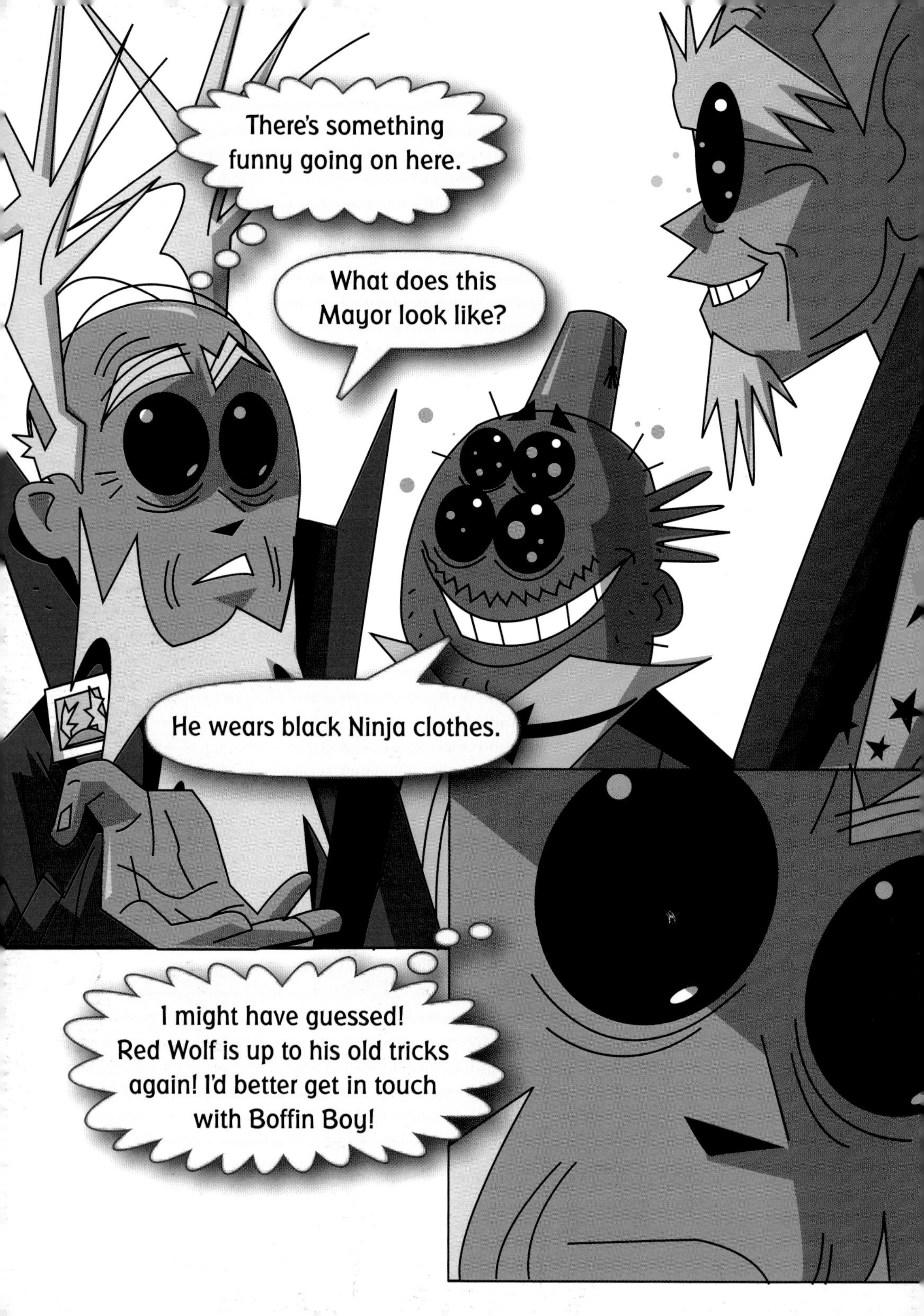
There's something funny going on here.
What does this Mayor look like?
He wears black Ninja clothes.
I might have guessed! Red Wolf is up to his old tricks again! I'd better get in touch with Boffin Boy!

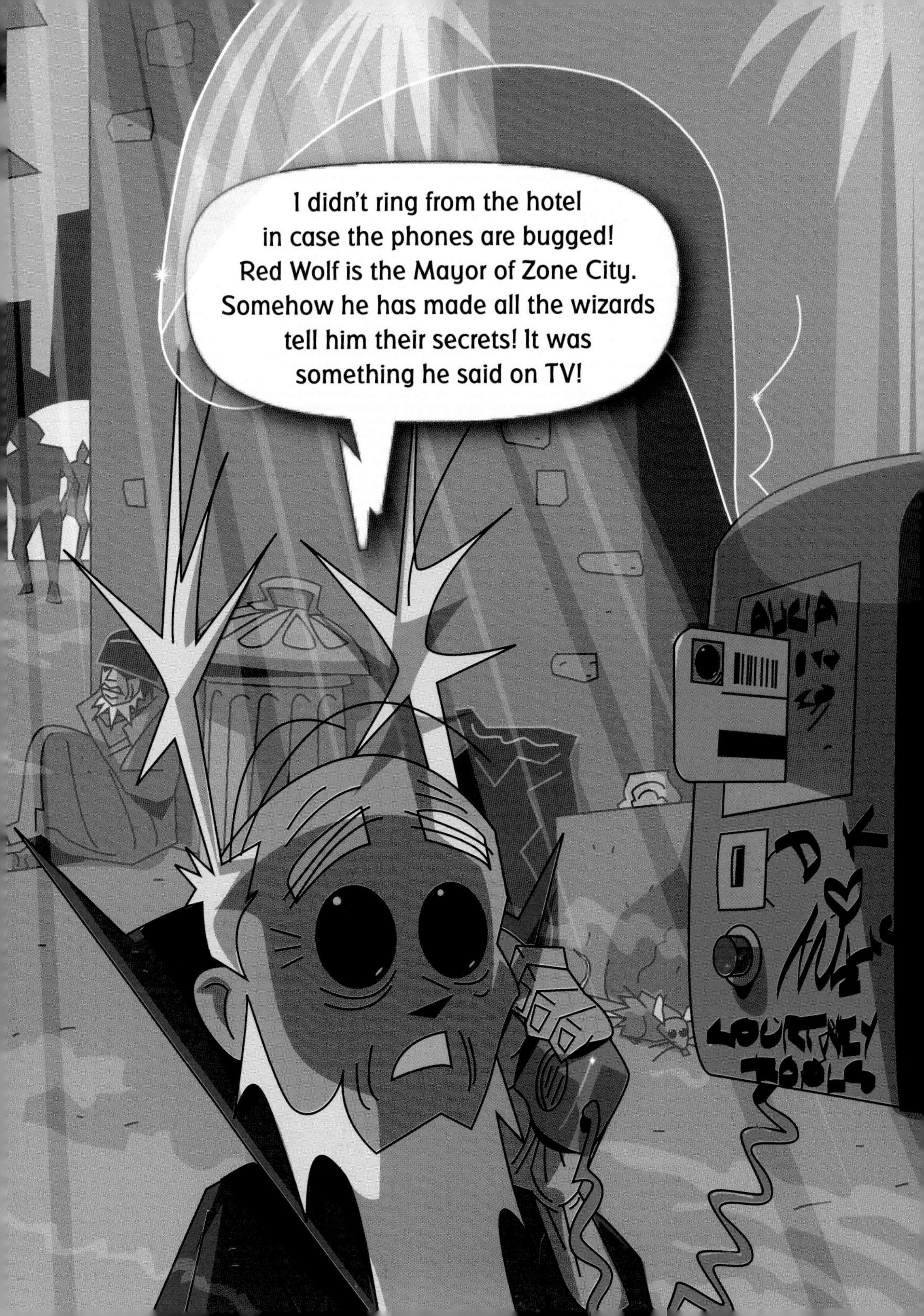
I didn't ring from the hotel in case the phones are bugged! Red Wolf is the Mayor of Zone City. Somehow he has made all the wizards tell him their secrets! It was something he said on TV!

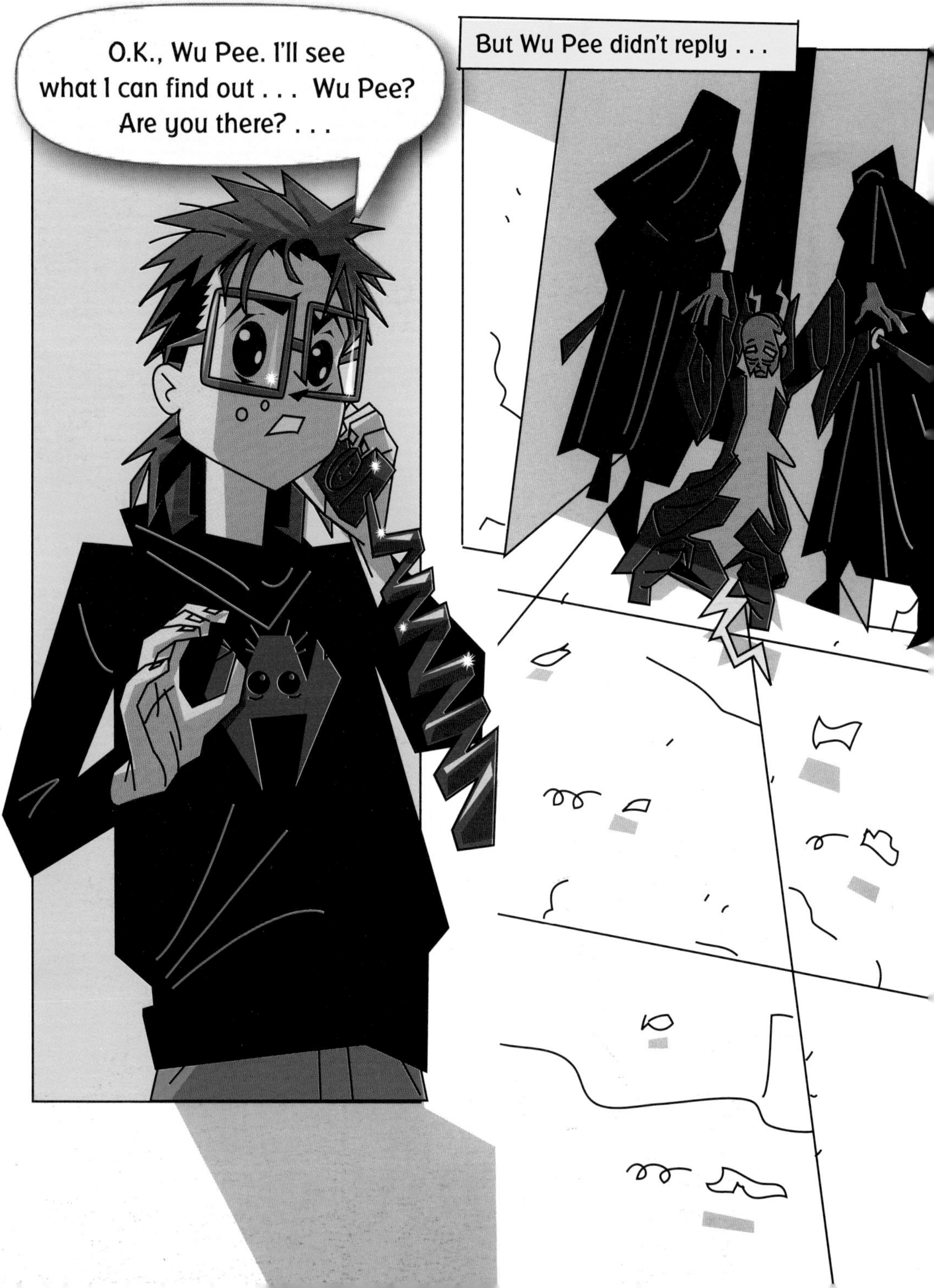
O.K., Wu Pee. I'll see what I can find out . . . Wu Pee? Are you there? . . .
But Wu Pee didn't reply . . .

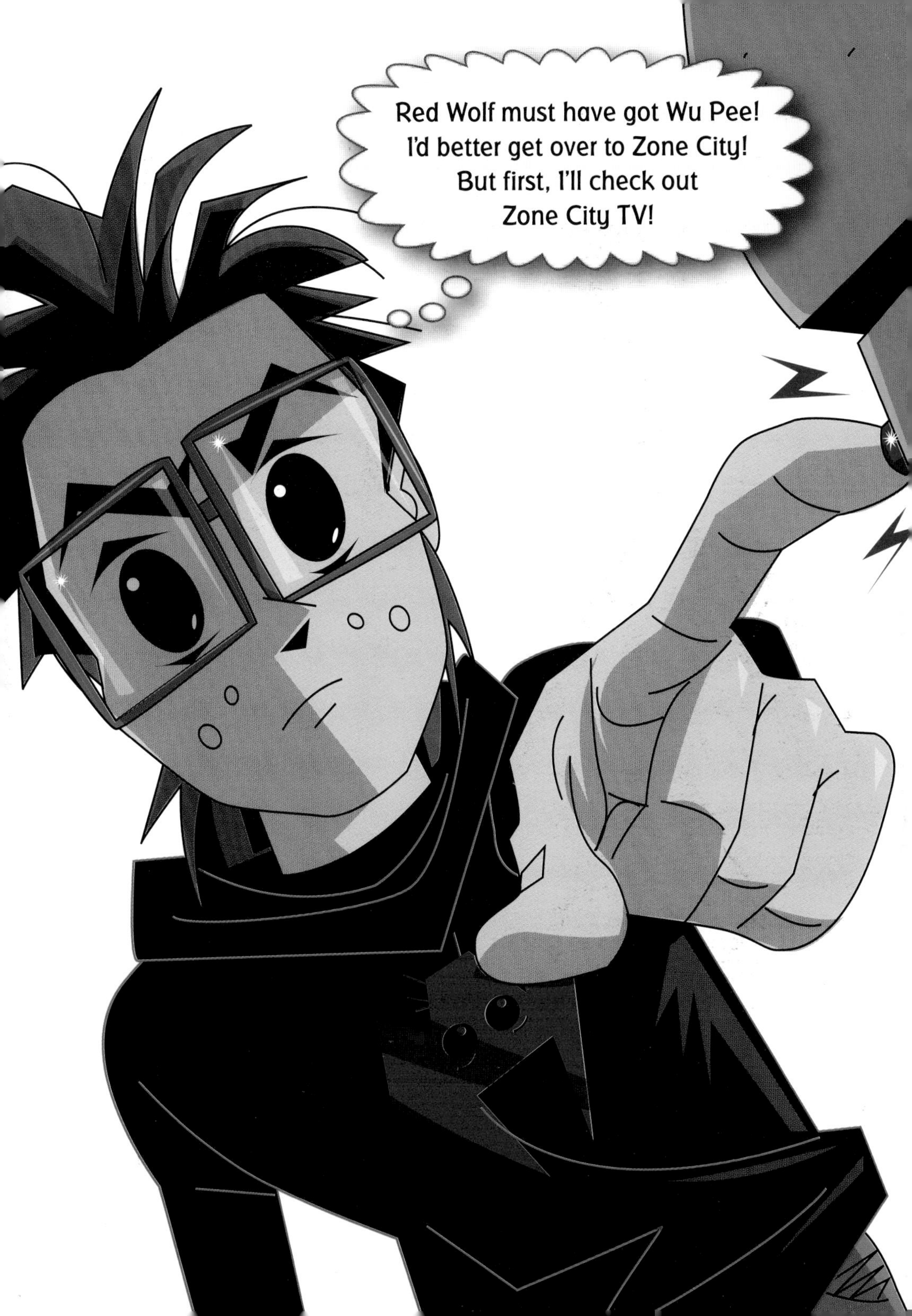
Red Wolf must have got Wu Pee! I'd better get over to Zone City! But first, I'll check out Zone City TV!

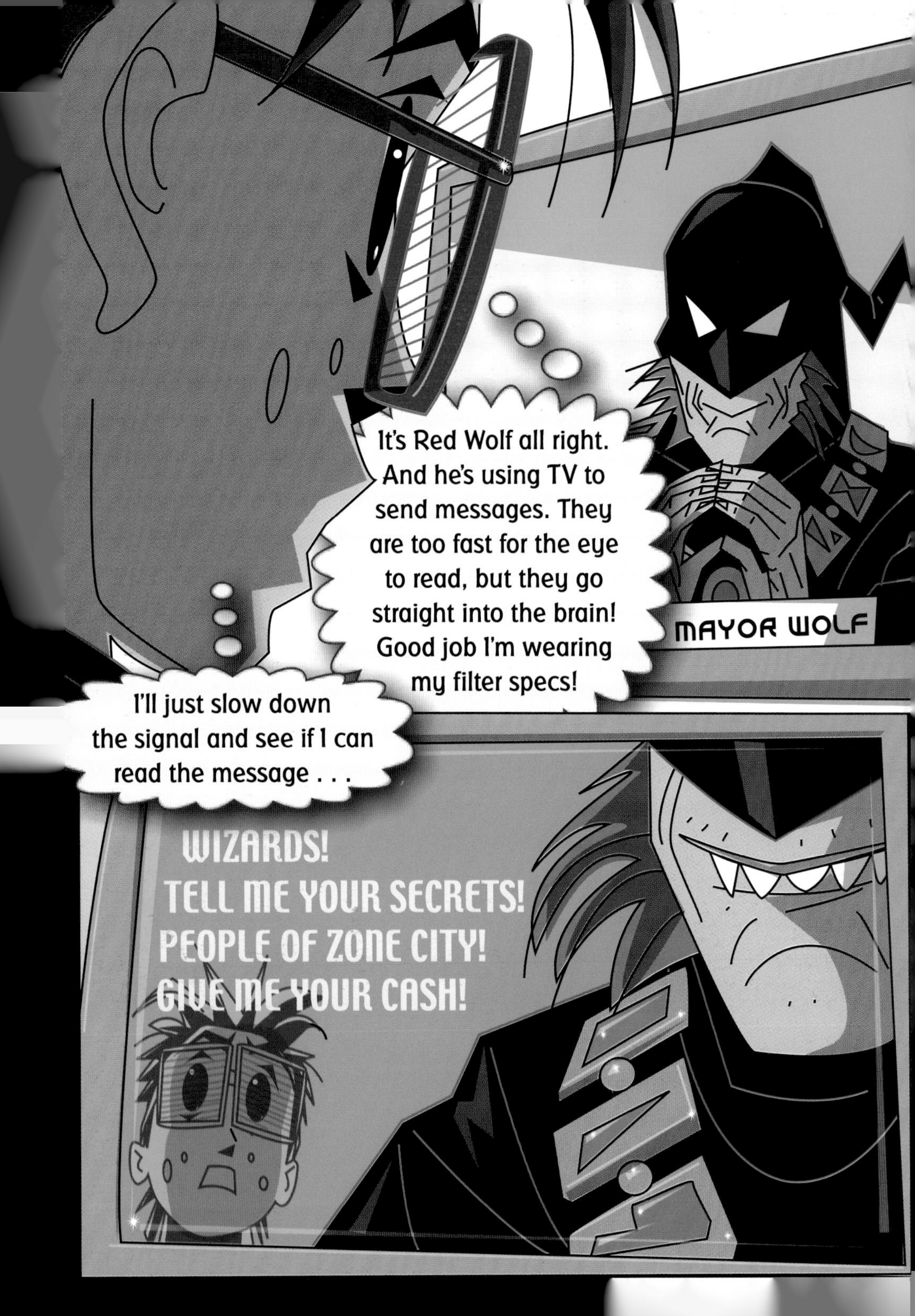
It's Red Wolf all right. And he's using TV to send messages. They are too fast for the eye to read, but they go straight into the brain! Good job I'm wearing my filter specs!
MAYOR WOLF
I'll just slow down the signal and see if I can read the message . . .
WIZARDS! TELL ME YOUR SECRETS! PEOPLE OF ZONE CITY! GIVE ME YOUR CASH!

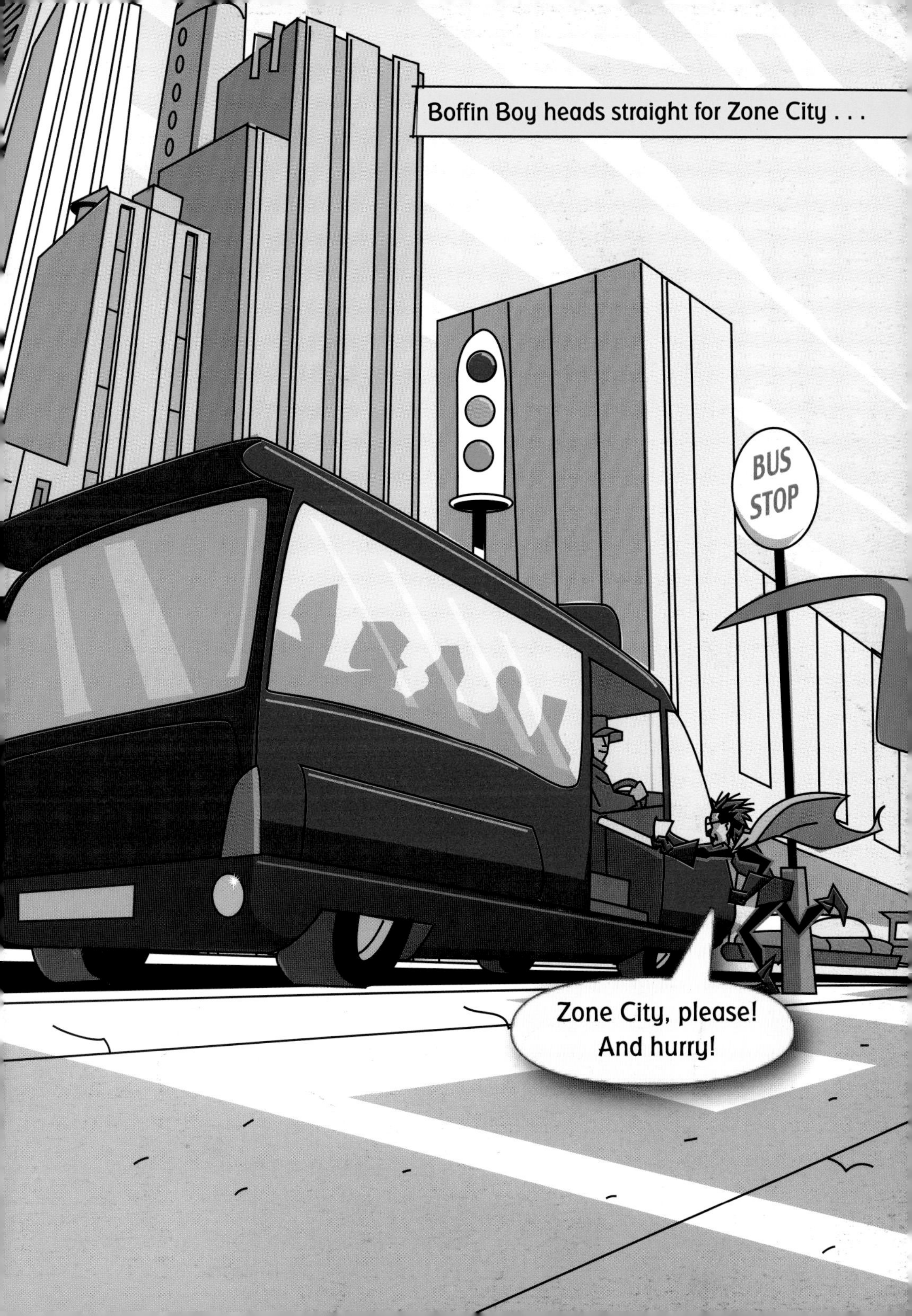
Boffin Boy heads straight for Zone City . . .
BUS STOP
Zone City, please! And hurry!

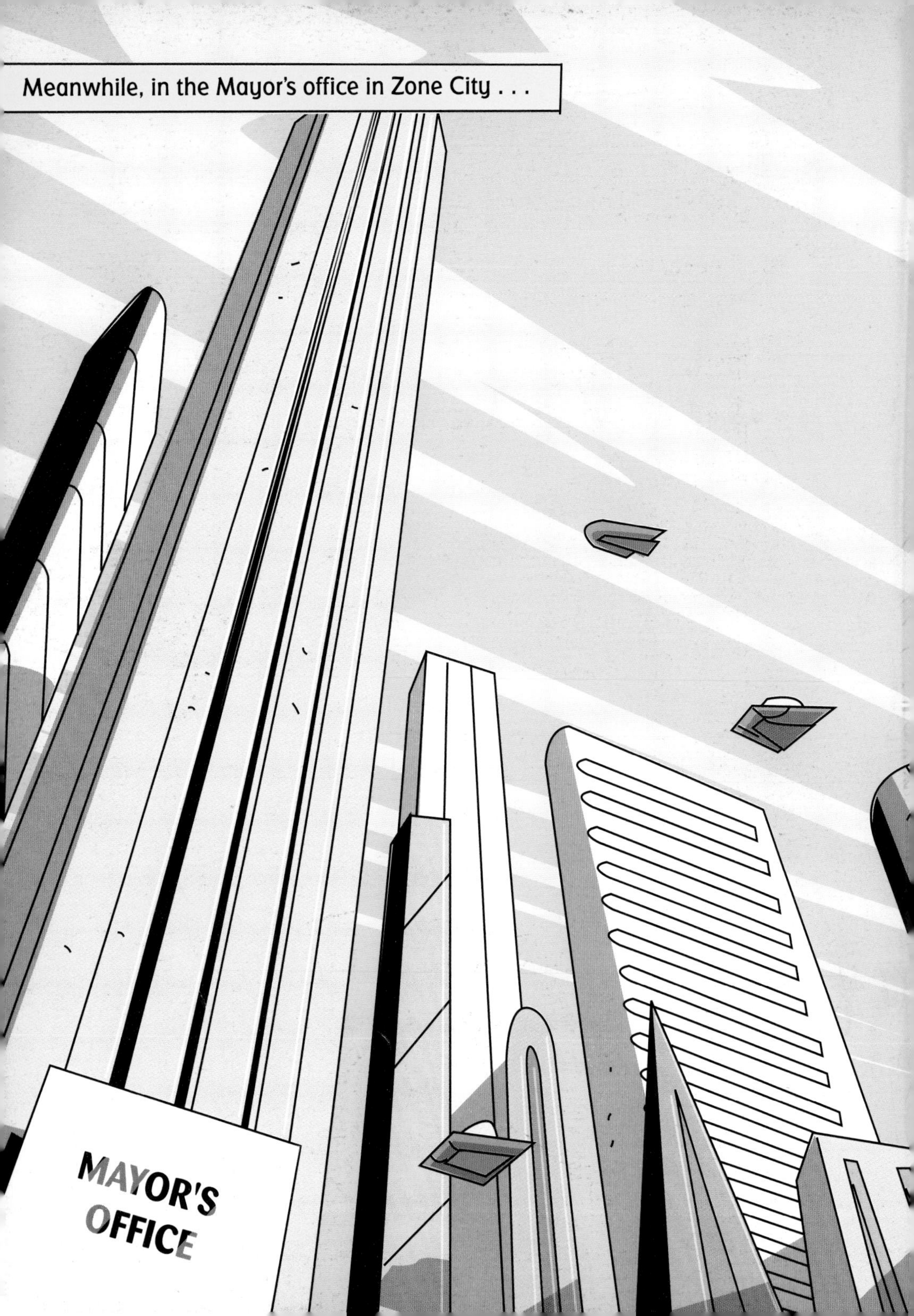
Meanwhile, in the Mayor's office in Zone City . . .
MAYOR'S
OFFICE

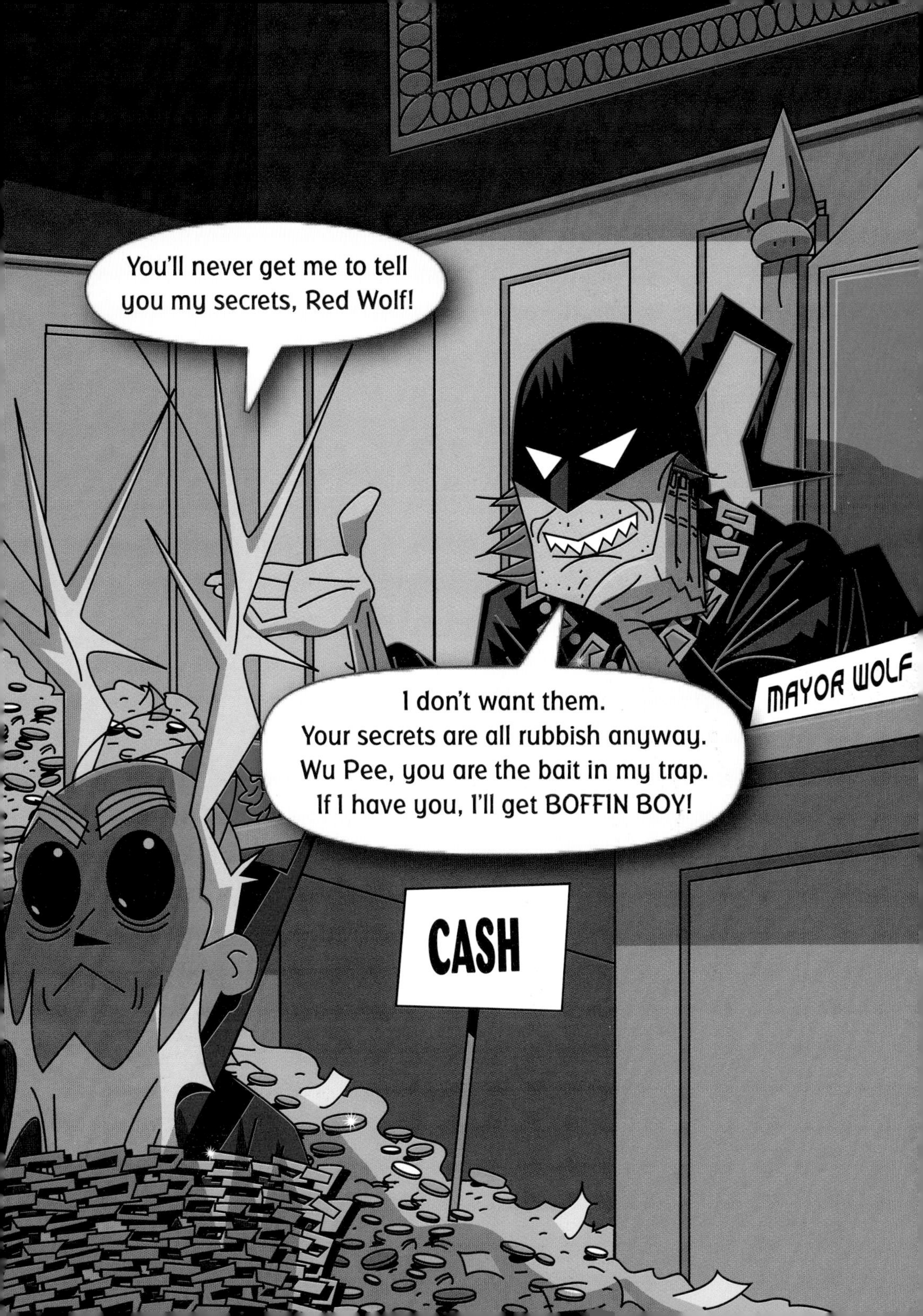
You'll never get me to tell you my secrets, Red Wolf!
I don't want them. Your secrets are all rubbish anyway. Wu Pee, you are the bait in my trap. If I have you, I'll get BOFFIN BOY!
MAYOR WOLF
CASH

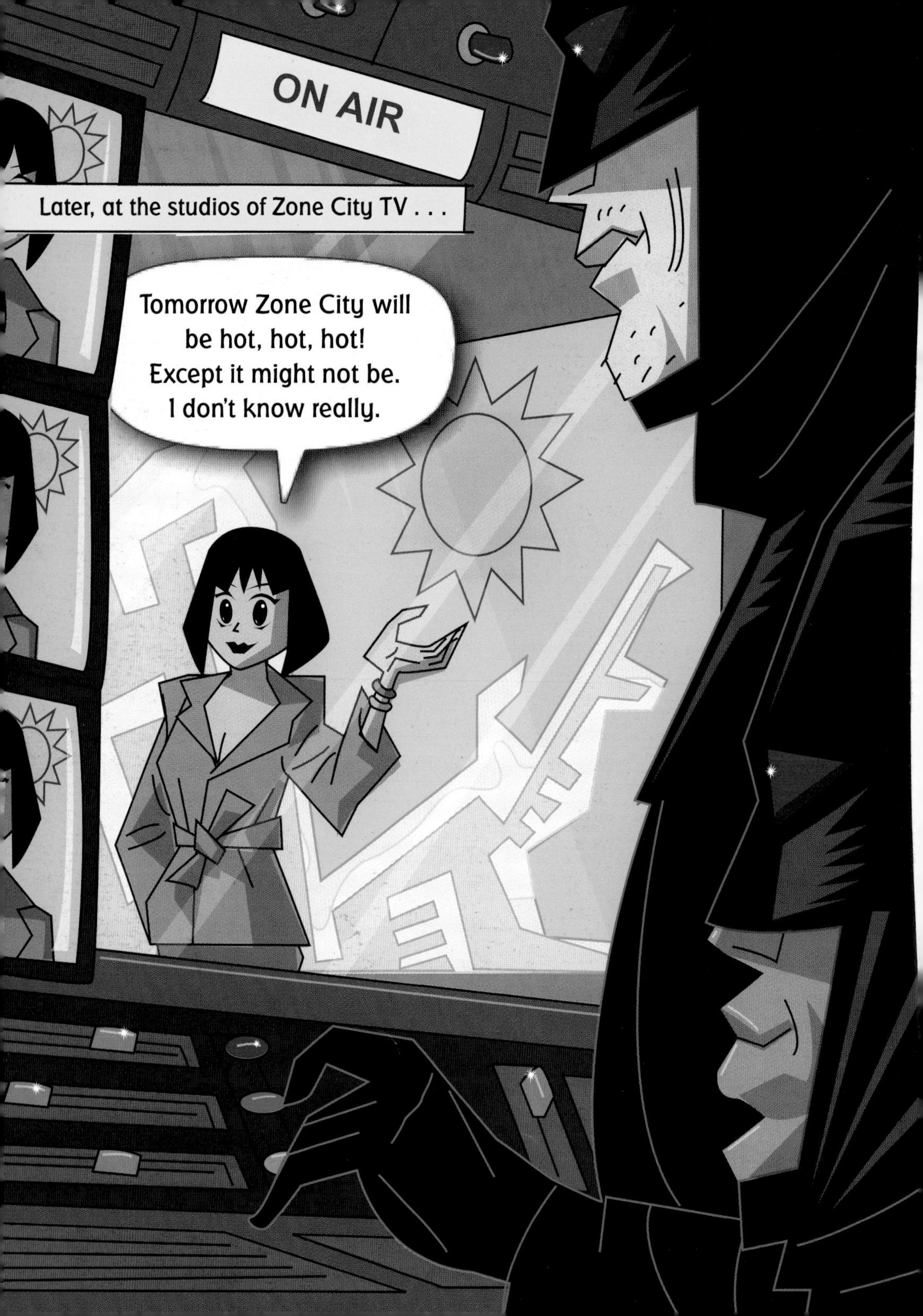
ON AIR
Later, at the studios of Zone City TV . . .
Tomorrow Zone City will be hot, hot, hot! Except it might not be. I don't know really.

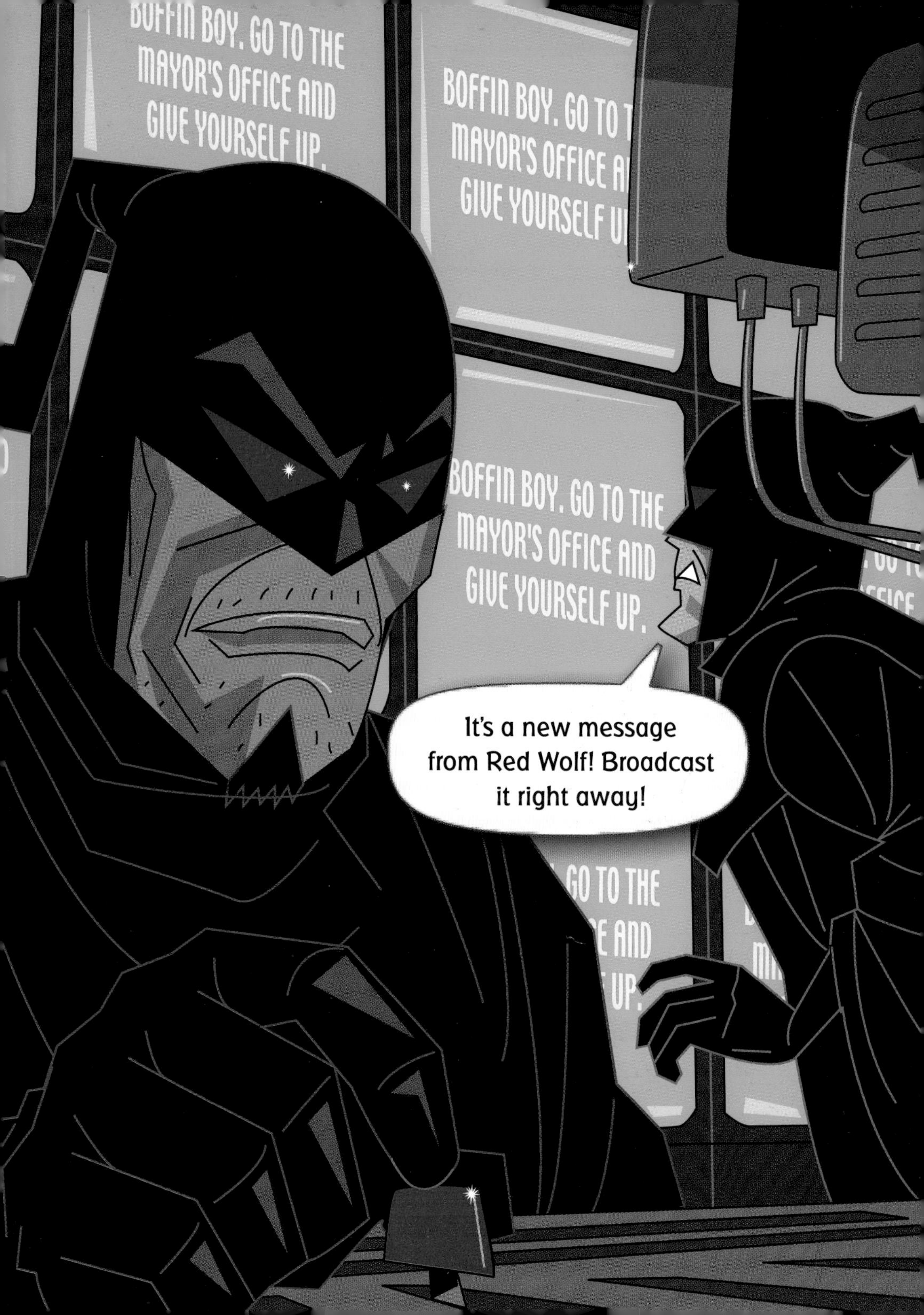
BOFFIN BOY. GO TO THE MAYOR'S OFFICE AND GIVE YOURSELF UP.
It's a new message from Red Wolf! Broadcast it right away!

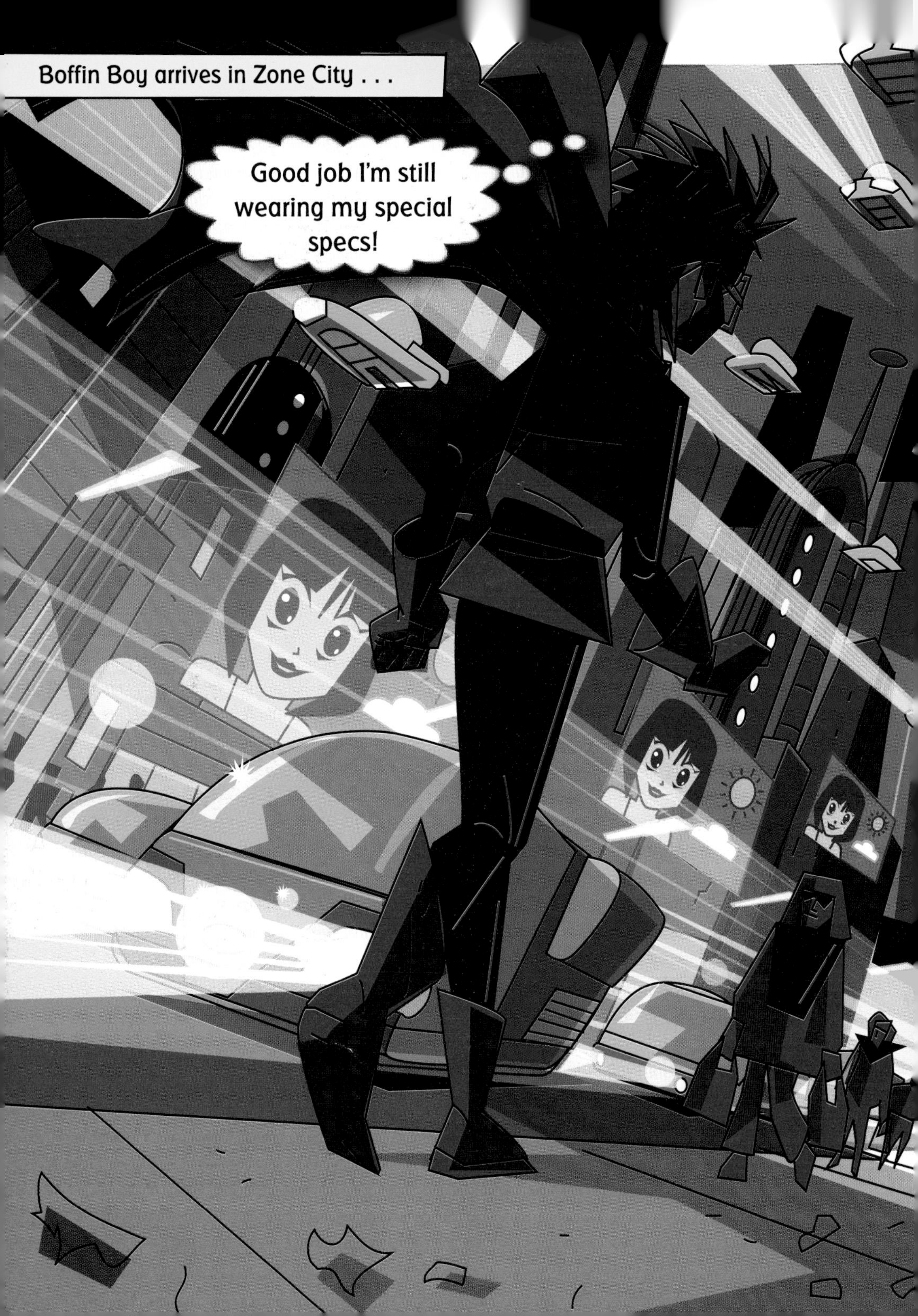
Boffin Boy arrives in Zone City . . .
Good job I'm still wearing my special specs!

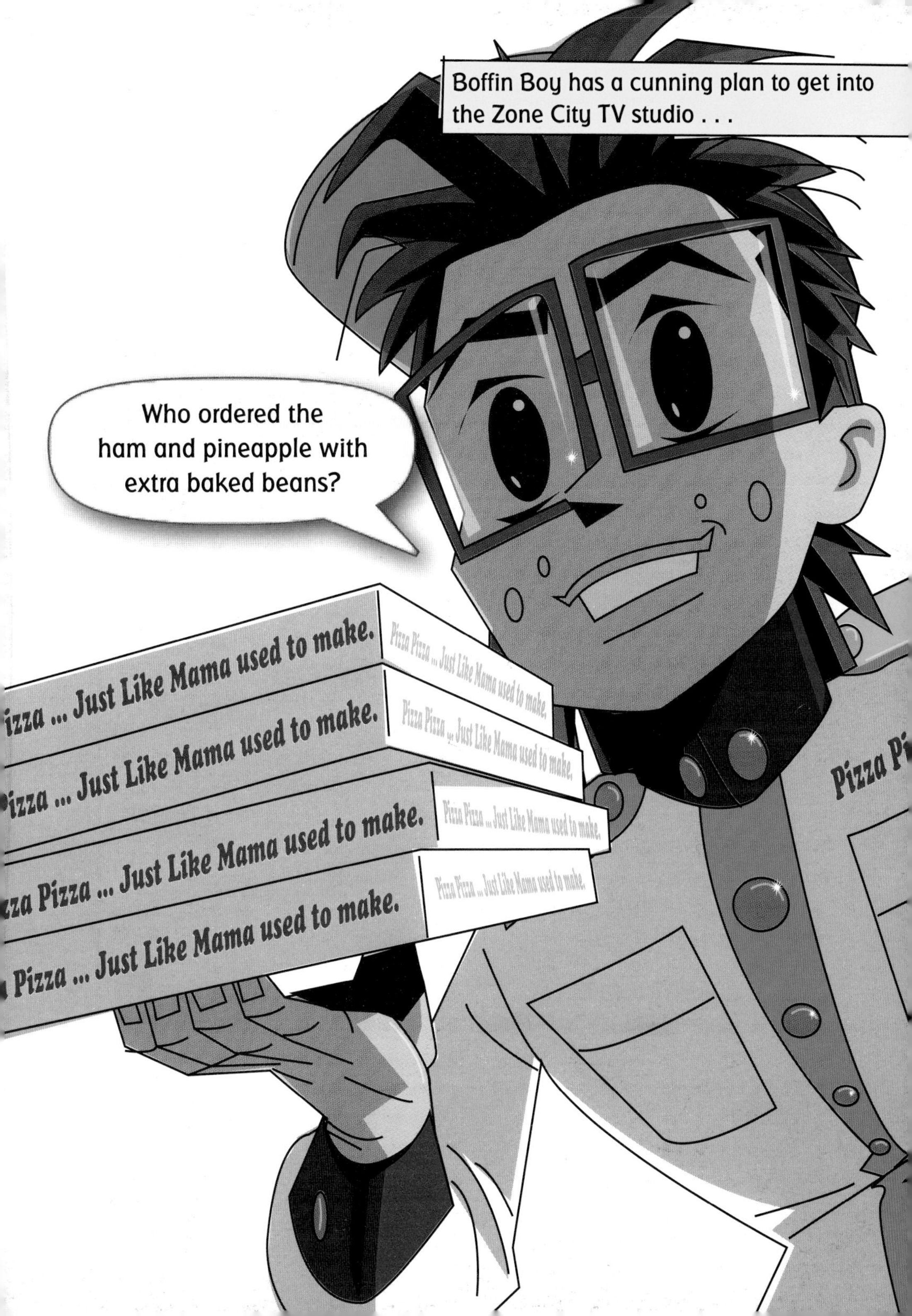
Boffin Boy has a cunning plan to get into the Zone City TV studio . . .
Who ordered the ham and pineapple with extra baked beans?
Pizza Pizza ... Just Like Mama used to make.
Pizza Pizza ... Just Like Mama used to make.
Pizza Pizza ... Just Like Mama used to make.
Pizza Pizza ... Just Like Mama used to make.

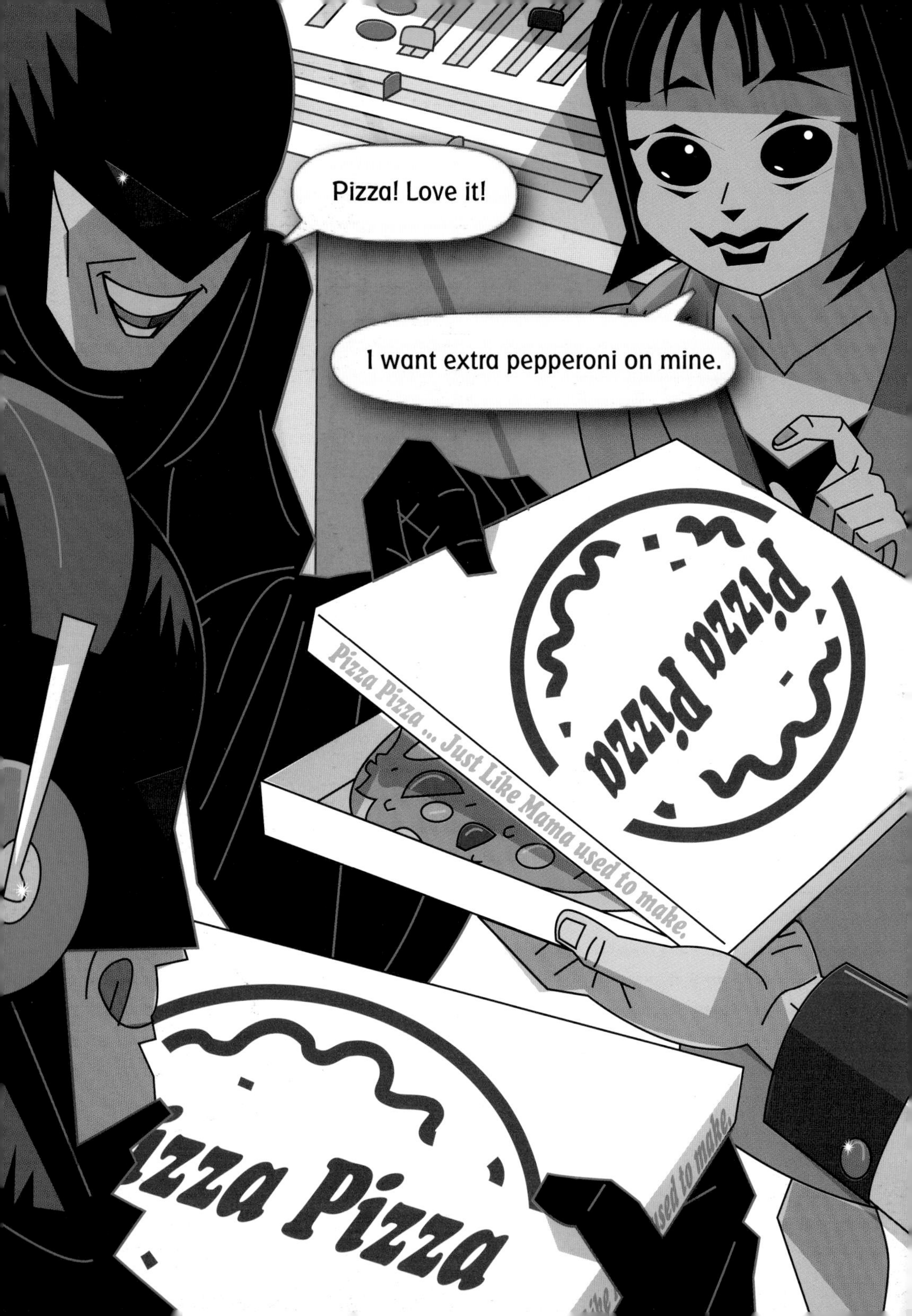
Pizza! Love it!
I want extra pepperoni on mine.
Pizza Pizza
Pizza Pizza ... Just Like Mama used to make.

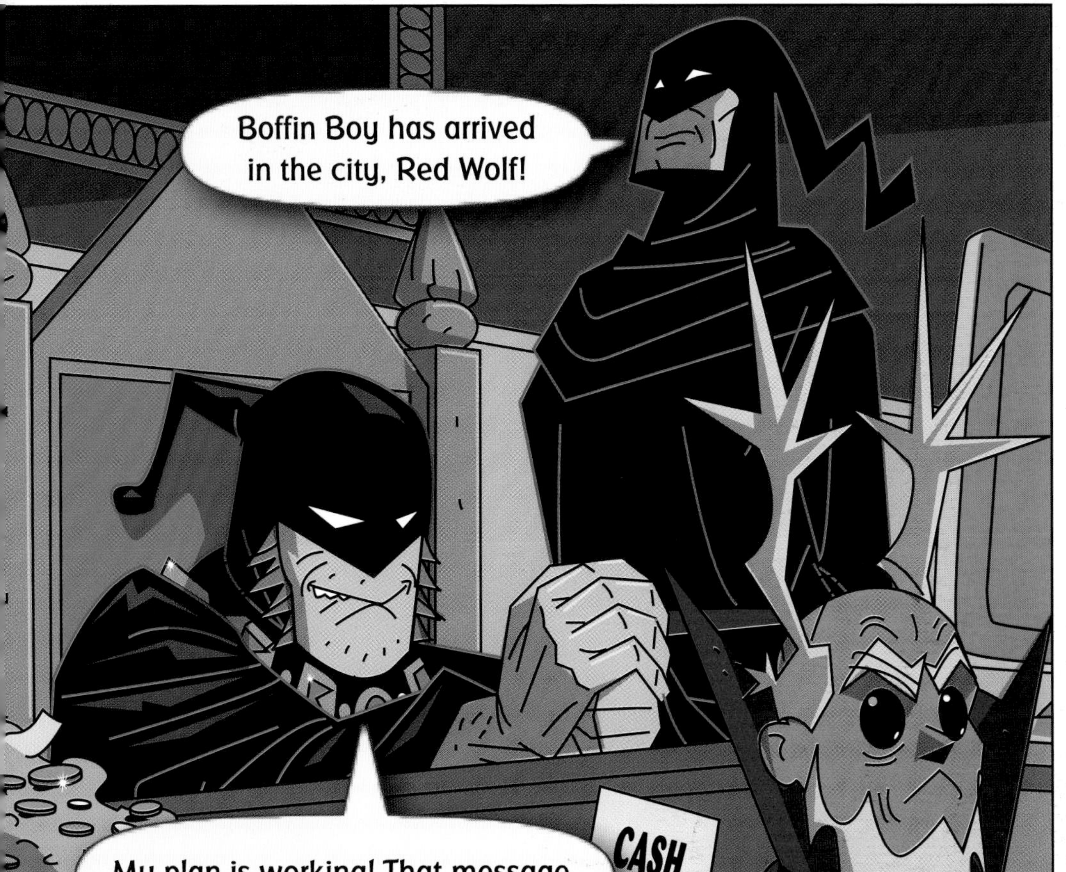
Boffin Boy has arrived in the city, Red Wolf!
My plan is working! That message should be going out now!
CASH

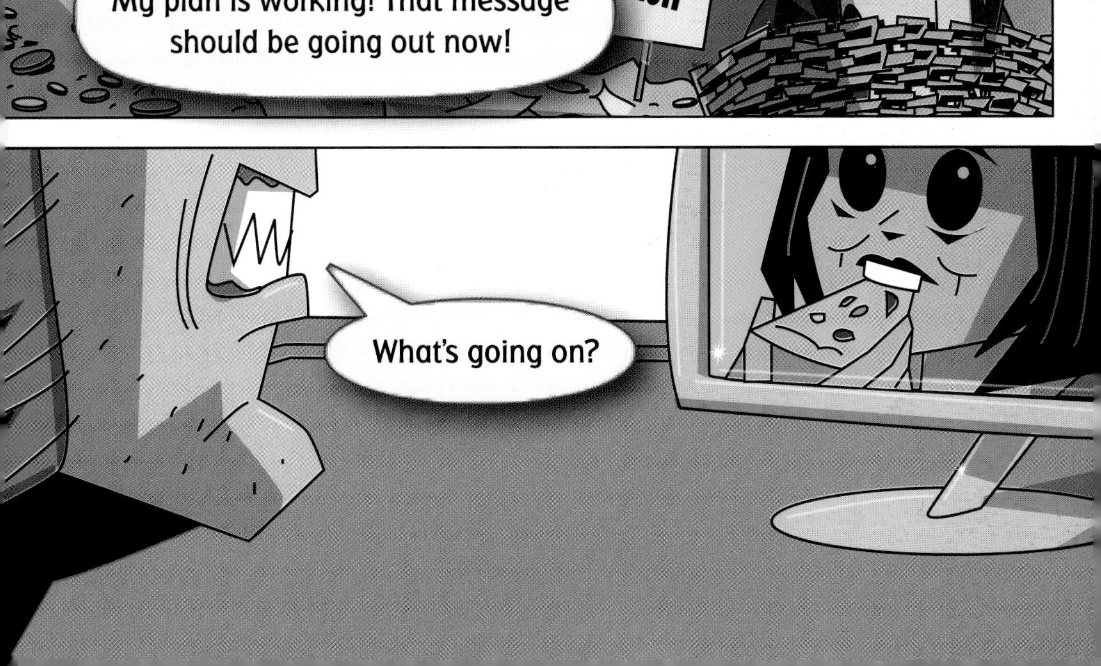
What's going on?

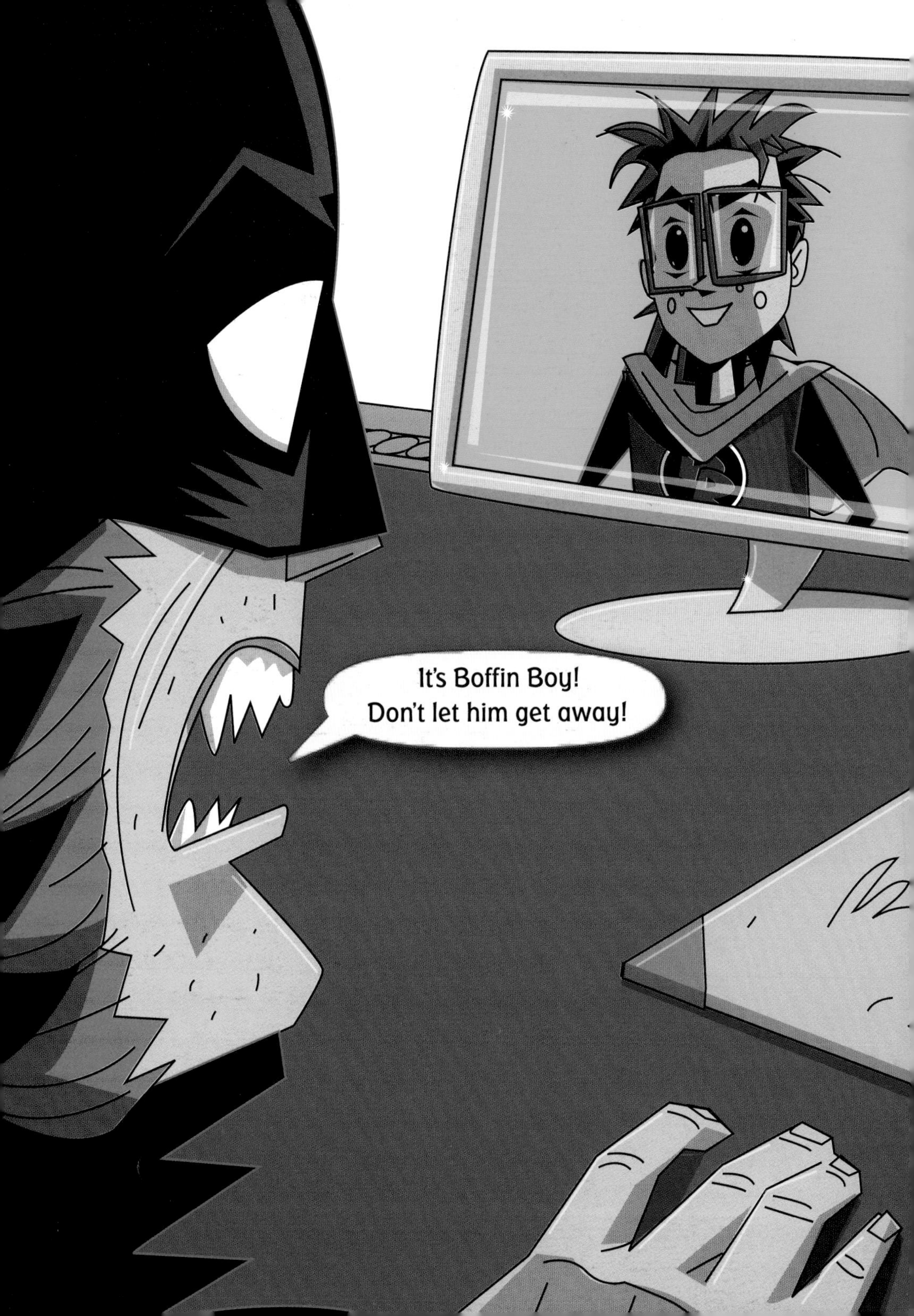
It's Boffin Boy!
Don't let him get away!

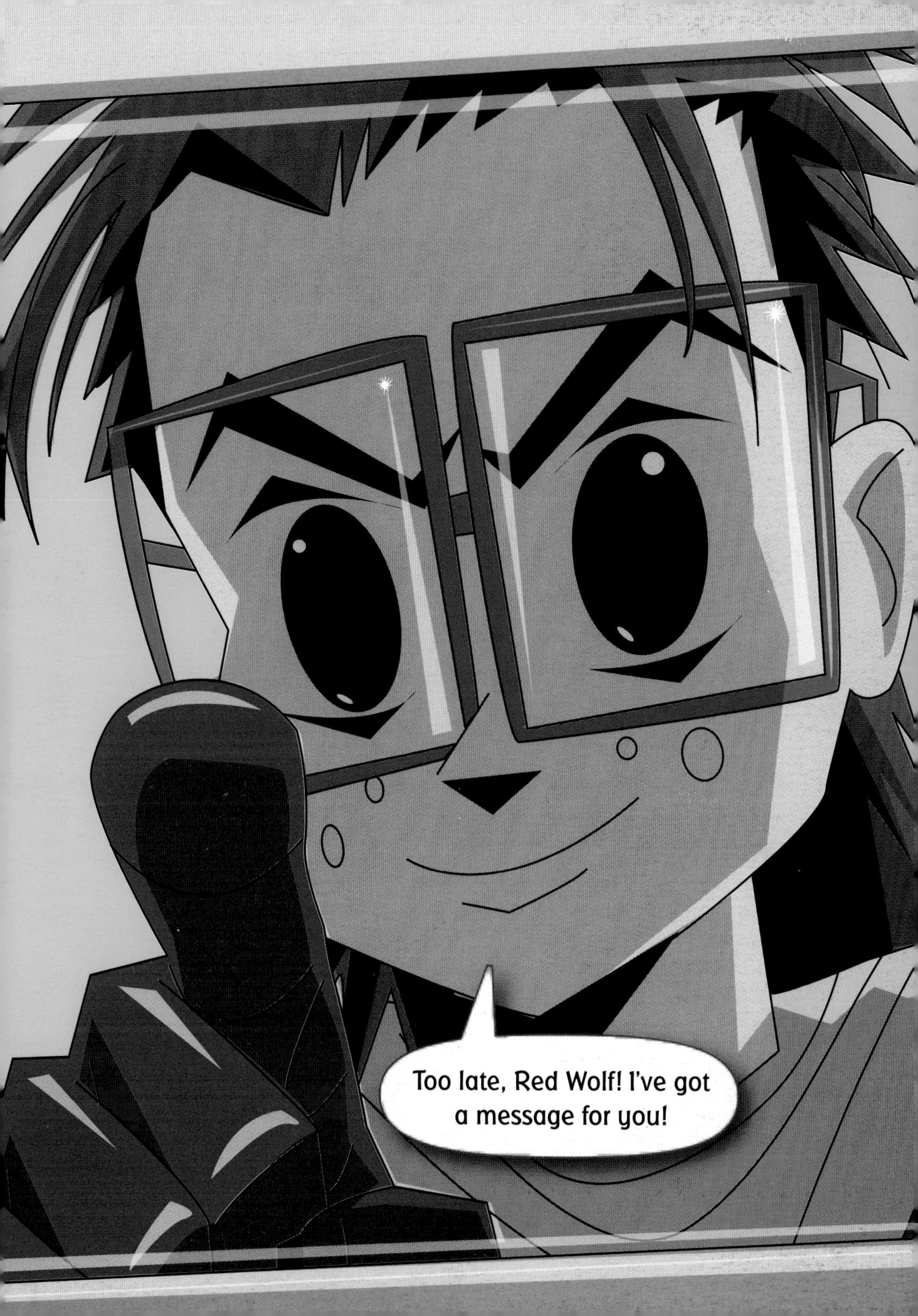
Too late, Red Wolf! I've got a message for you!

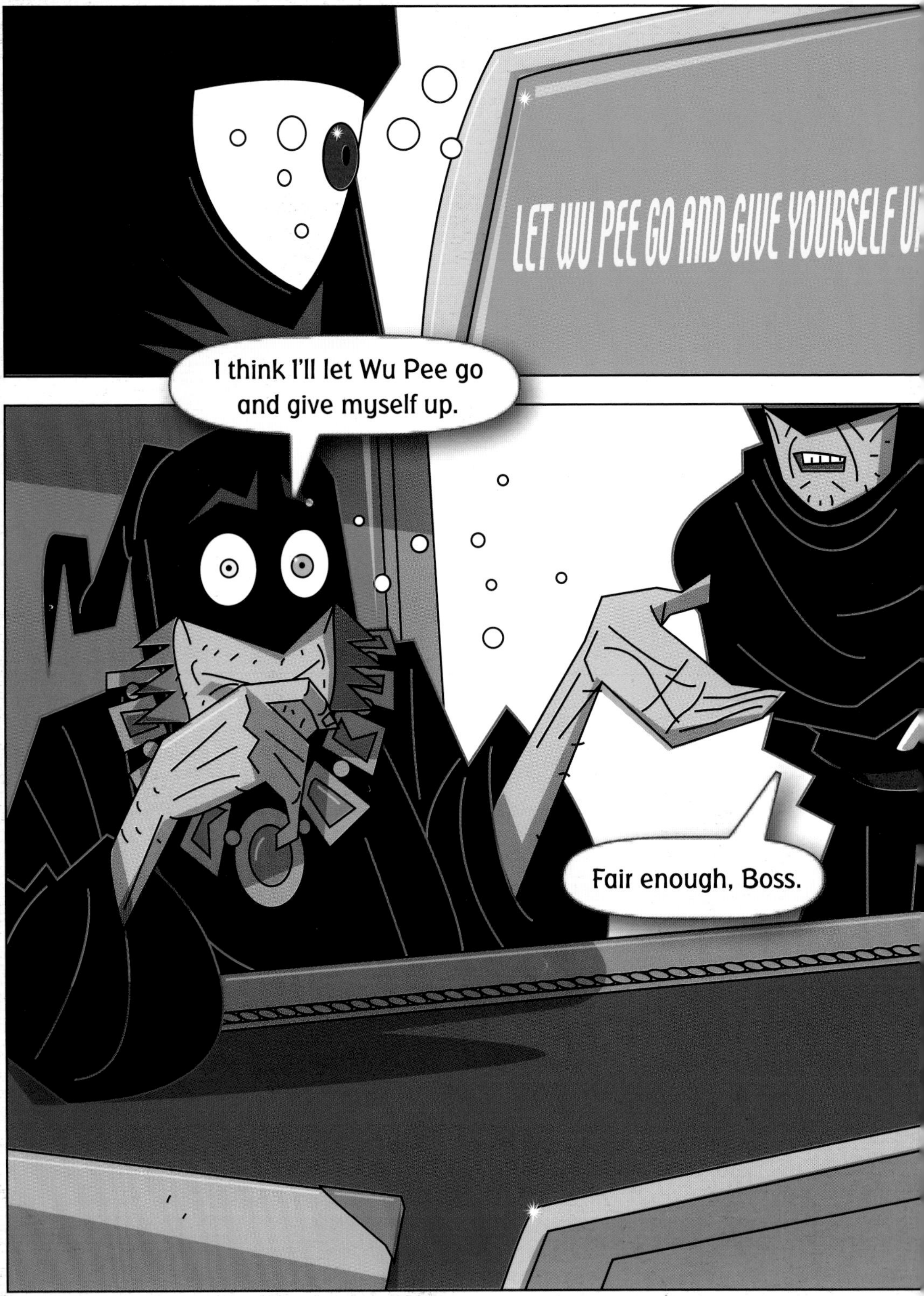
LET WU PEE GO AND GIVE YOURSELF U
I think I'll let Wu Pee go and give myself up.
Fair enough, Boss.

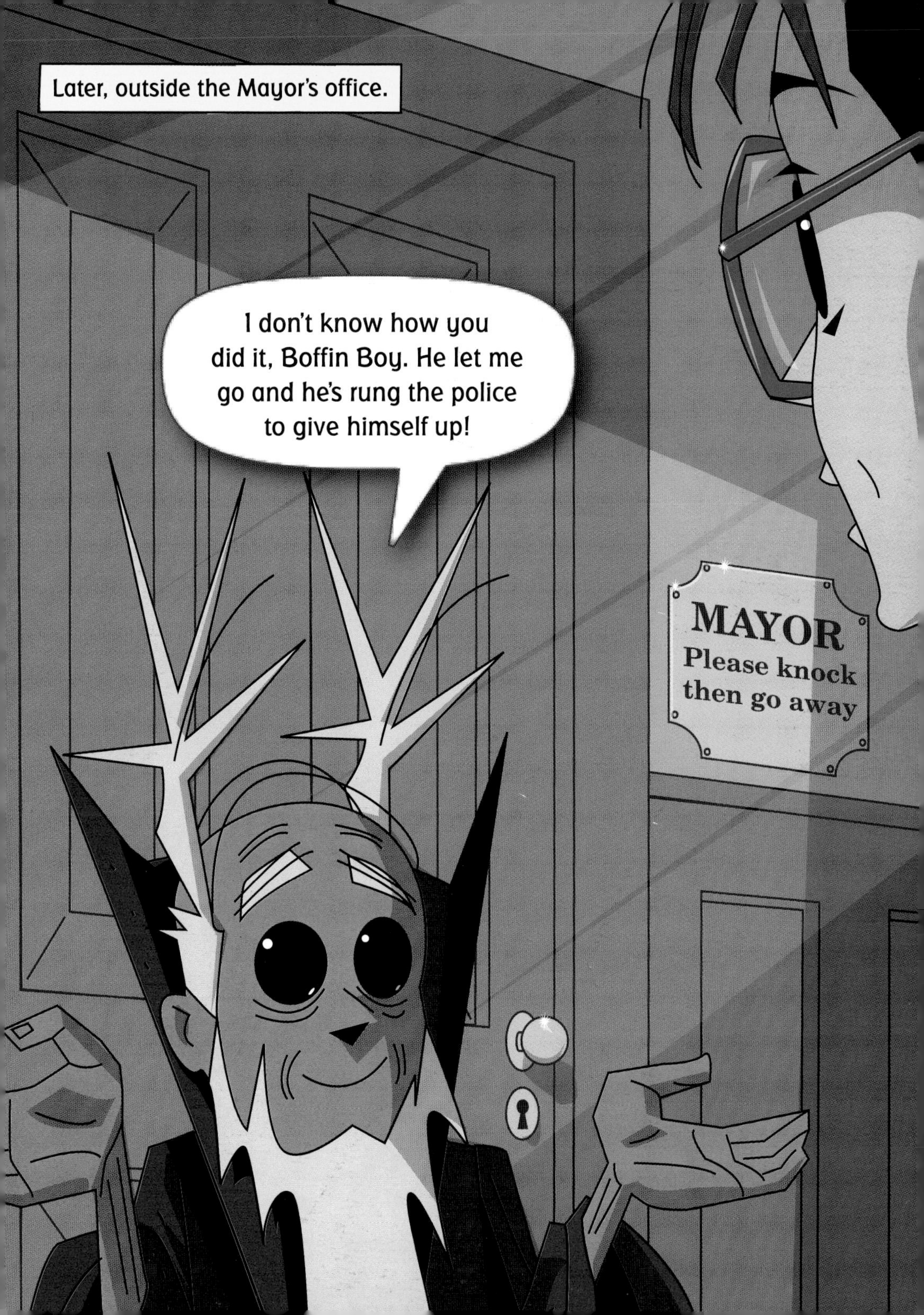
Later, outside the Mayor's office.
I don't know how you did it, Boffin Boy. He let me go and he's rung the police to give himself up!
MAYOR
Please knock then go away

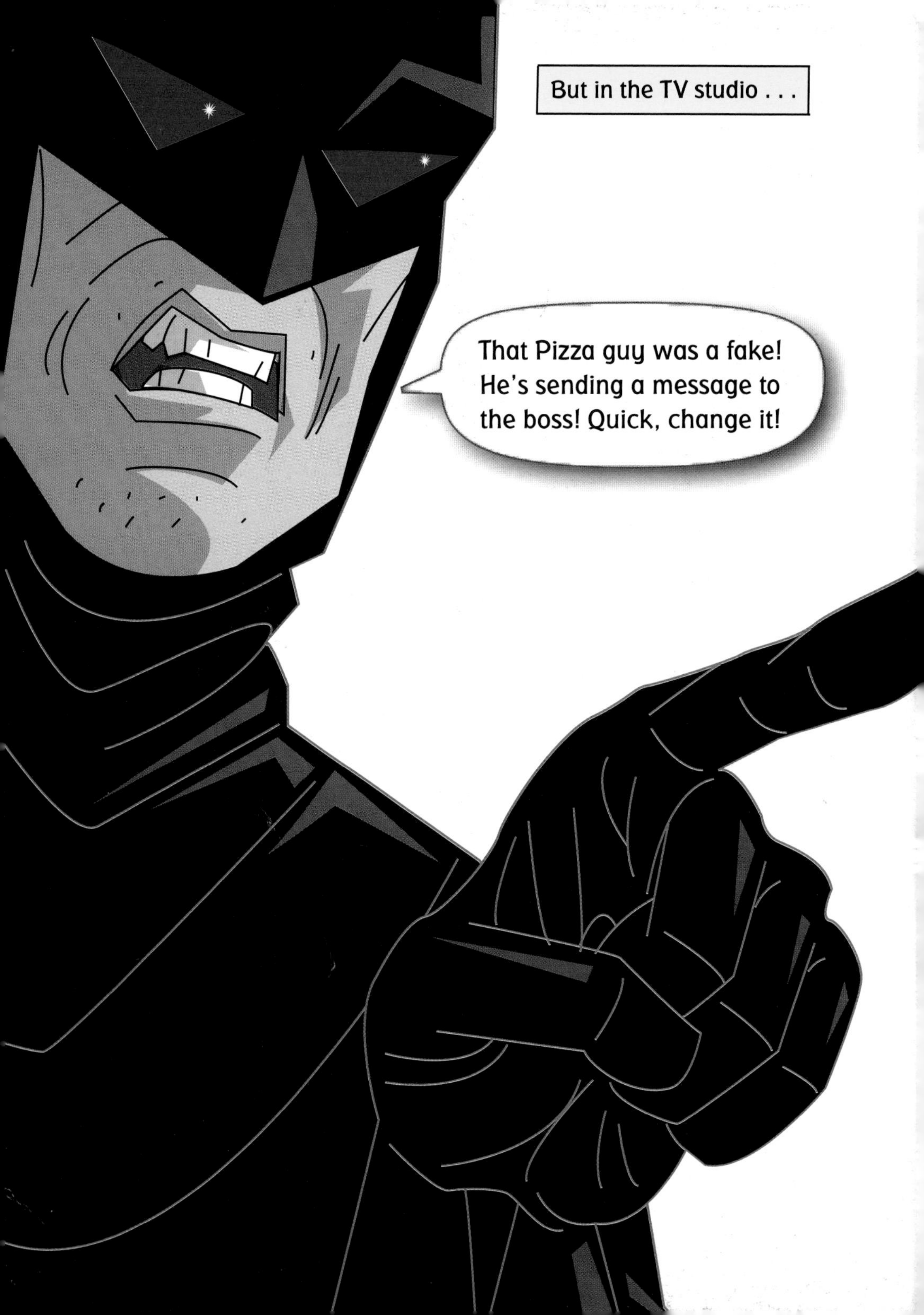
But in the TV studio . . .
That Pizza guy was a fake! He's sending a message to the boss! Quick, change it!

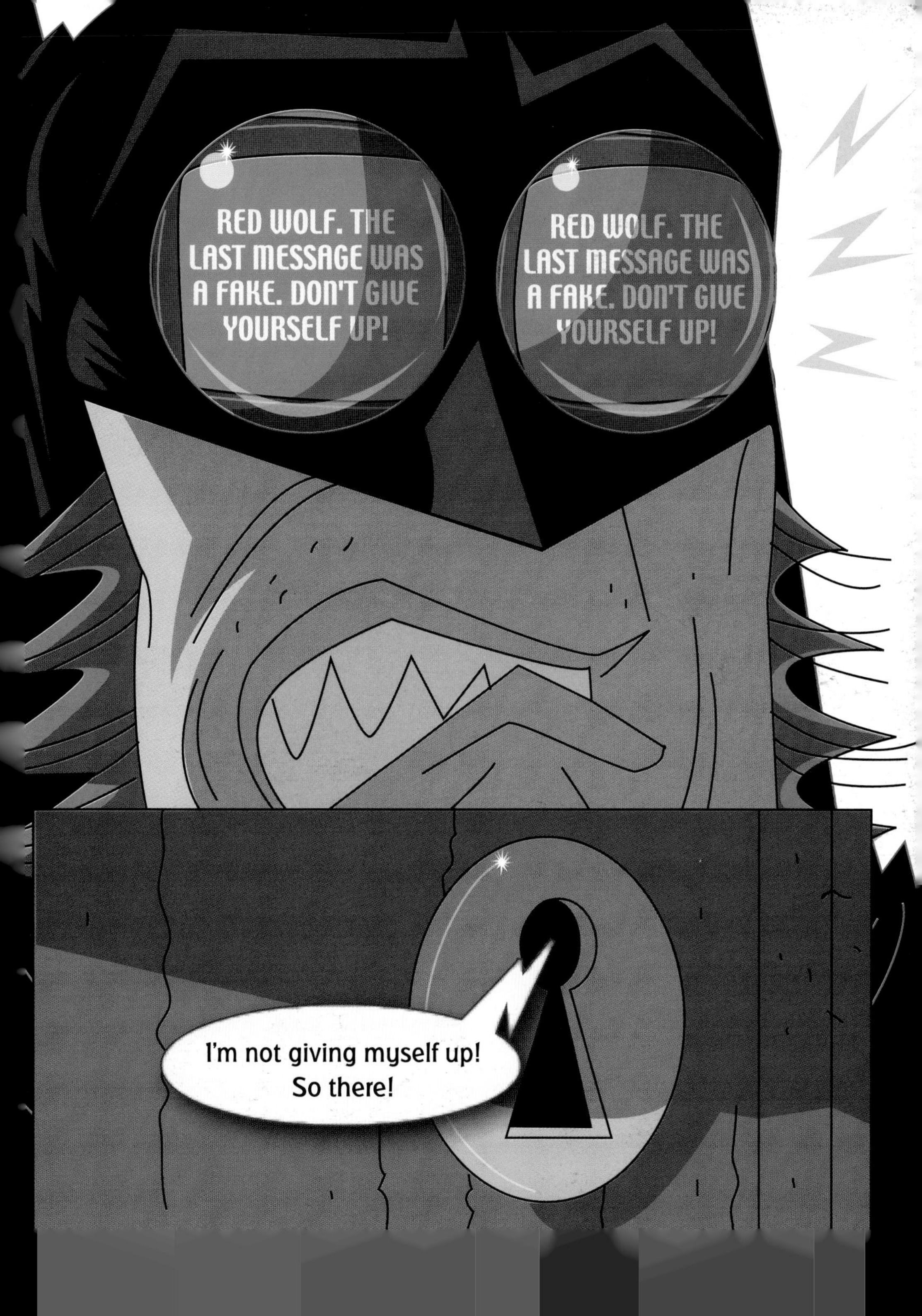
RED WOLF. THE LAST MESSAGE WAS A FAKE. DON'T GIVE YOURSELF UP!
RED WOLF. THE LAST MESSAGE WAS A FAKE. DON'T GIVE YOURSELF UP!
I'm not giving myself up! So there!

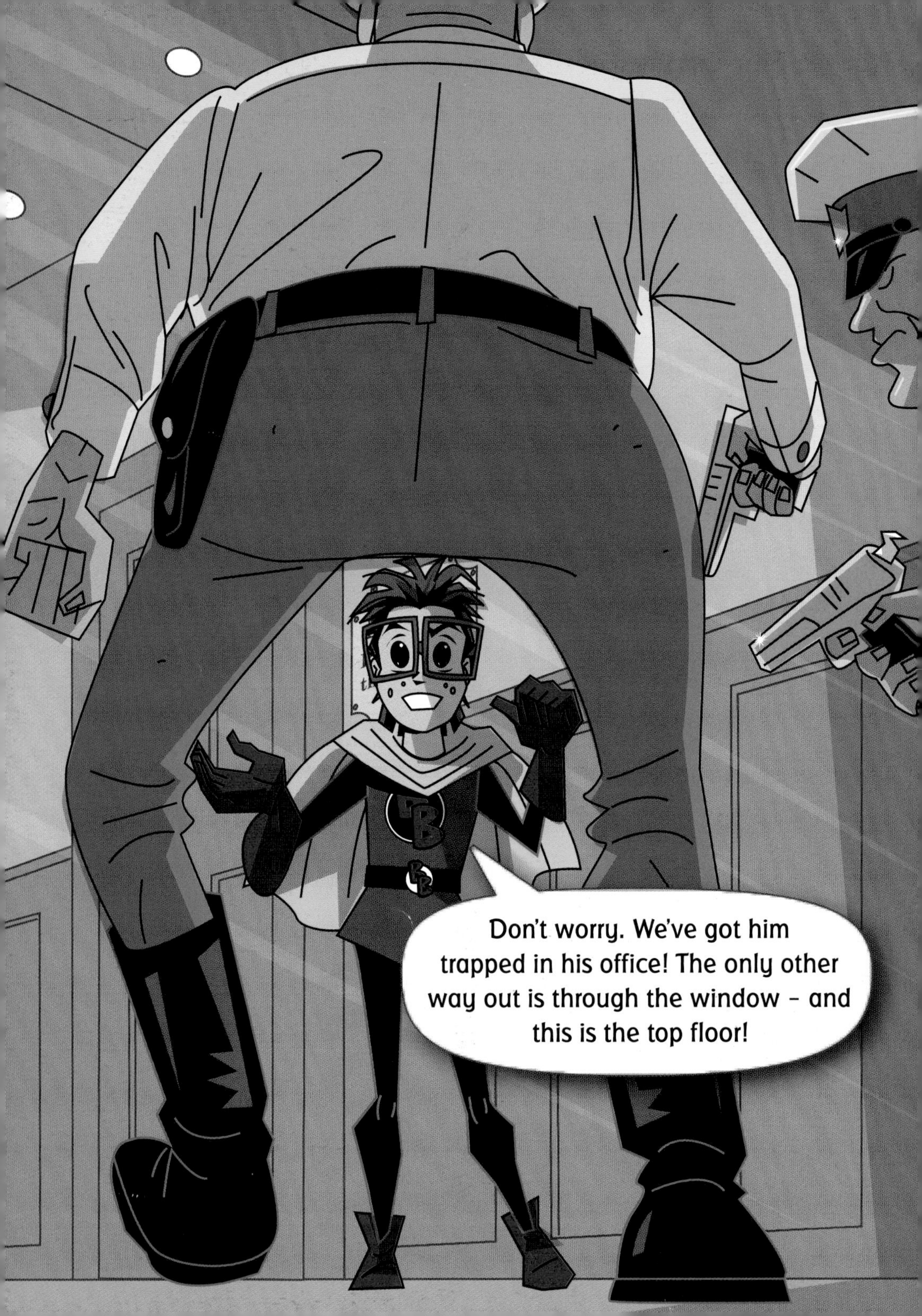
Don't worry. We've got him trapped in his office! The only other way out is through the window – and this is the top floor!

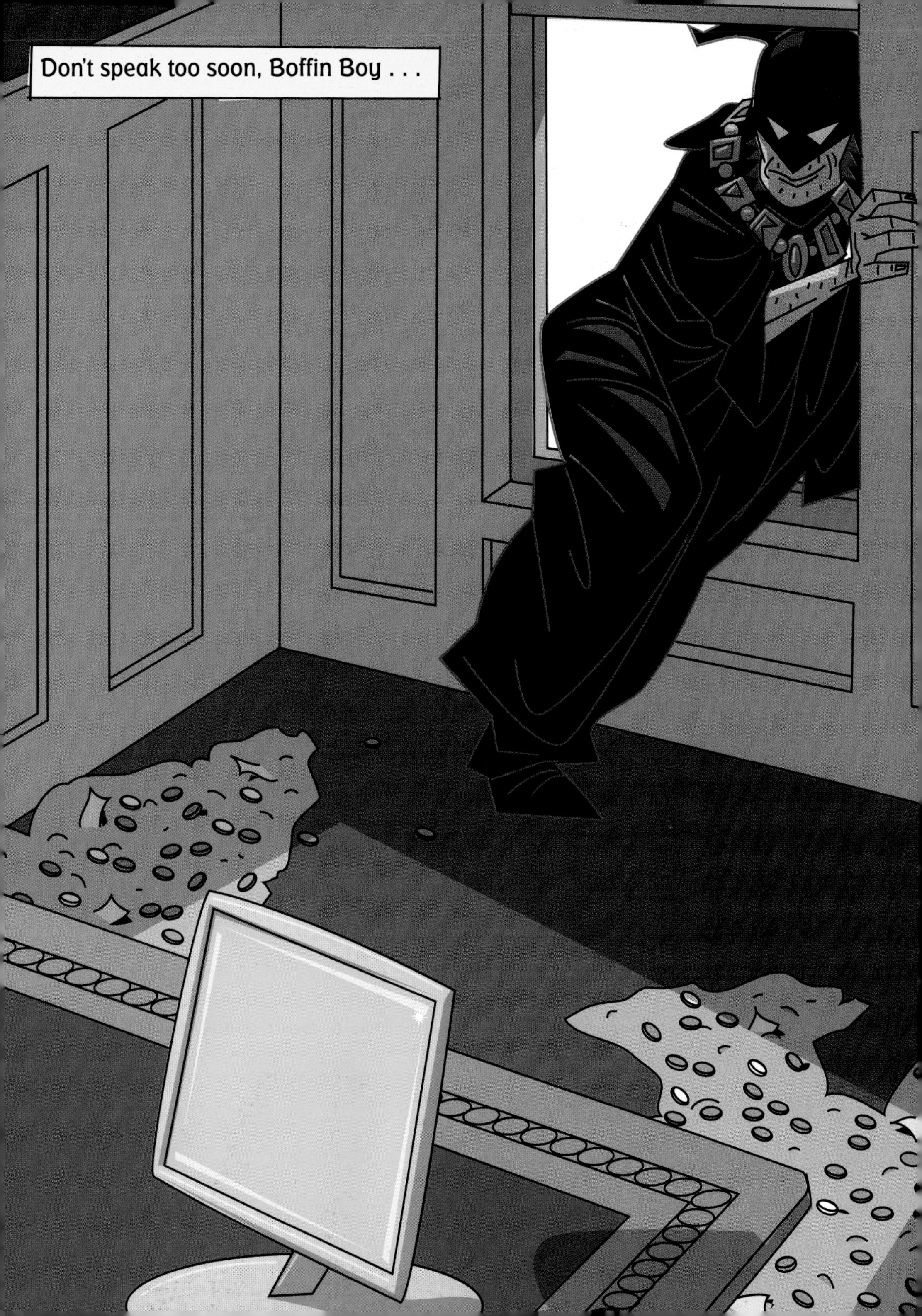
Don't speak too soon, Boffin Boy . . .

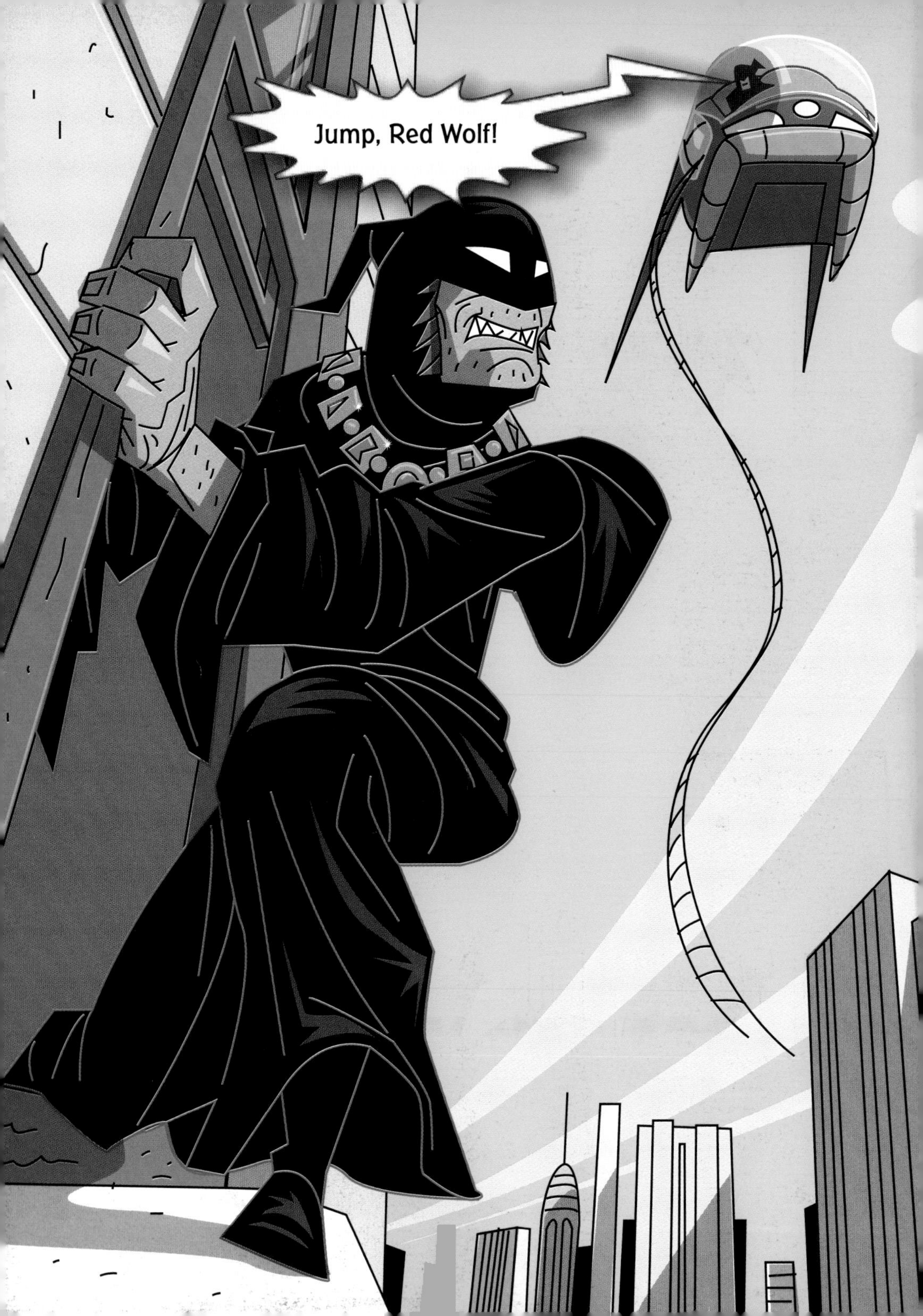
Jump, Red Wolf!

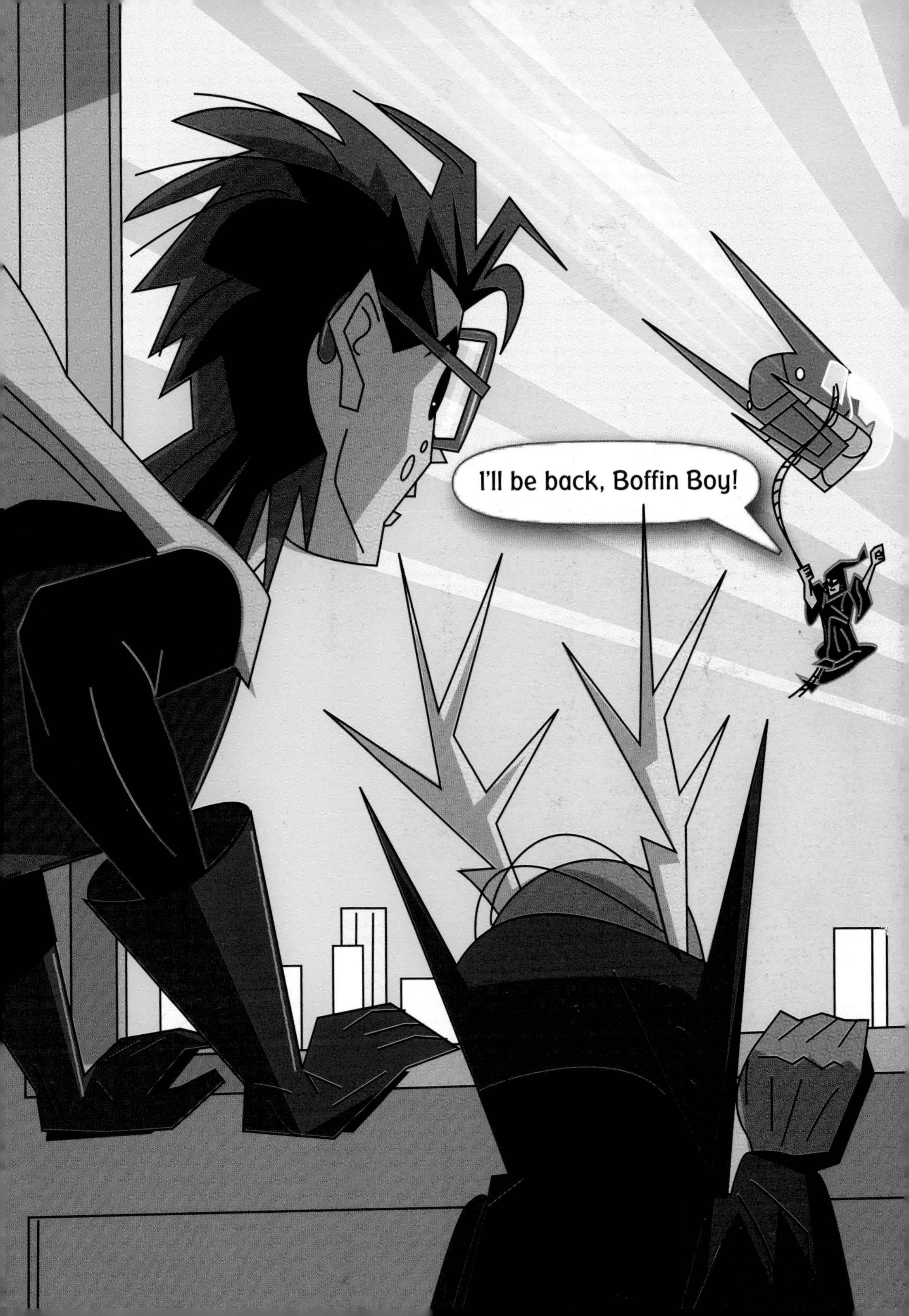
I'll be back, Boffin Boy!

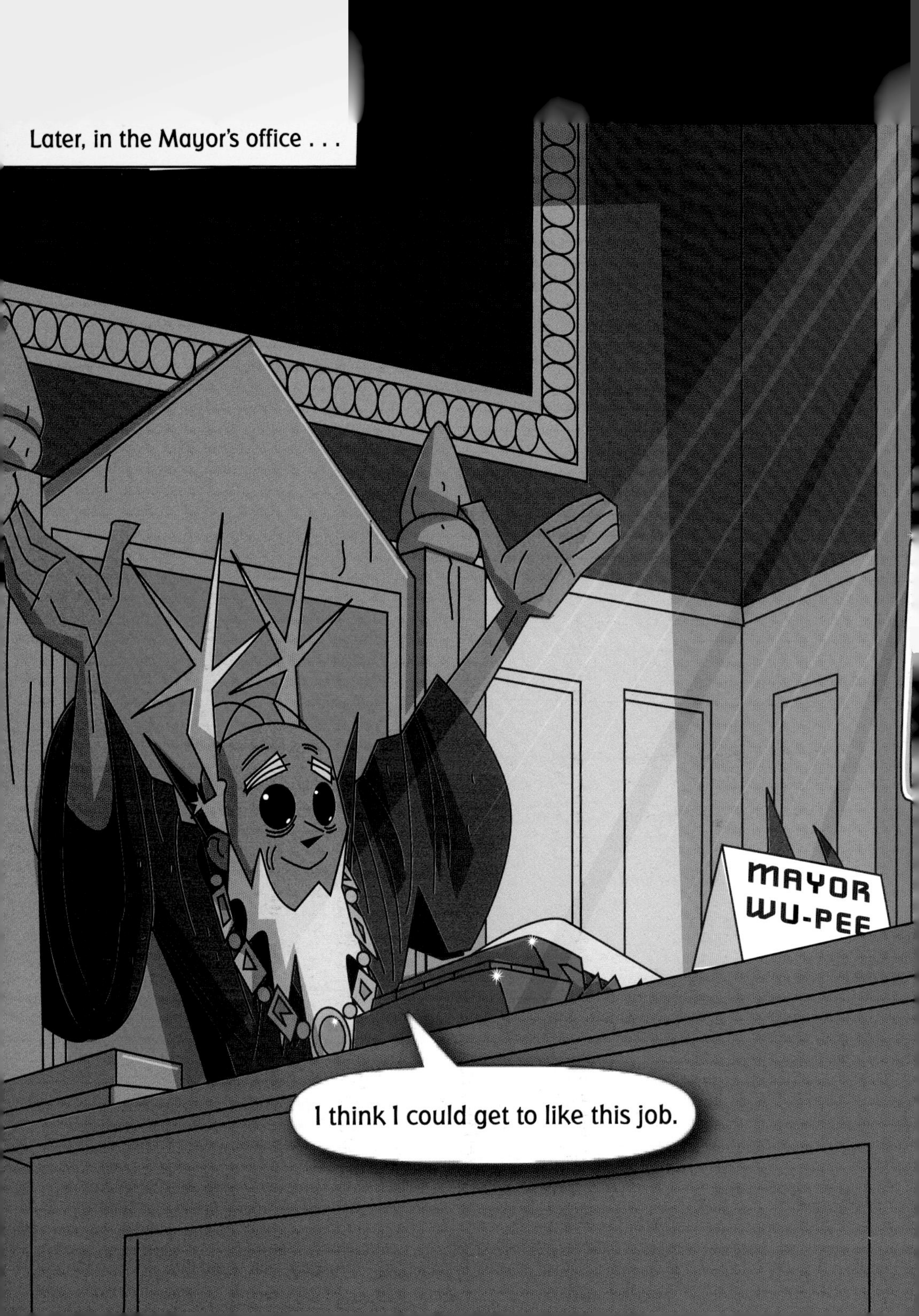
Later, in the Mayor's office . . .
MAYOR WU-PEE
I think I could get to like this job.

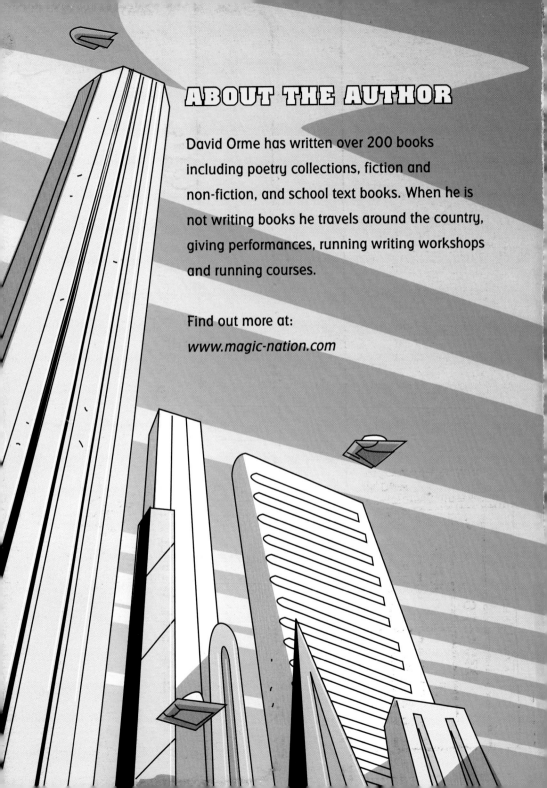

ABOUT THE AUTHOR

David Orme has written over 200 books including poetry collections, fiction and non-fiction, and school text books. When he is not writing books he travels around the country, giving performances, running writing workshops and running courses.

Find out more at:
www.magic-nation.com